Surprised
By Love

Books by Jasmine Cresswell

Surprised
By Love

Jasmine Cresswell

SPEAKING VOLUMES, LLC

NAPLES, FLORIDA

2012

Surprised By Love

Originally published under the name Jasmine Craig

ISBN 978-1-61232-823-2

Chapter One

CATHRYN PUSHED HERSELF away from the desk, stretching to ease the cramped muscles in her neck. Her body ached from too many hours spent poring over financial data sheets, but her mind remained infuriatingly active.

Sometimes, if she worked really late at the client's office, she was able to fall asleep as soon as her head touched the pillow. More often, though, however late she worked and however tired she was, the memories of Robert would crowd in, making sleep impossible.

Standing up to stretch again, she felt a sensation akin to panic when she realized that this was going to be another one of the nights when sleep would prove impossible. The memory of Robert smiling tenderly as she walked down the aisle of the church thrust itself into her mind and stayed there with cruel, unbearable clarity.

She slammed shut the record books she had been examining and slipped her calculator and a few crucial papers into her briefcase. There was no point in trying to do any more work tonight. Accounting required total concentration, and she had effectively lost hers.

Cathryn pulled on the gray linen jacket that matched her gray skirt and glanced down at her watch. Nine o'clock. The offices of Consolidated Vision had been quiet since five and deserted since seven. She hoped she would meet one of the security guards before she left the building. He might know where she could find a gym or an indoor swimming pool that was still open to the public at this time of night. She had discovered that if working late didn't succeed in banishing the too-vivid memories, physical exhaustion occasionally did the trick.

She was putting away the last of the client's confidential files when she became aware that someone was watching her. She swung around quickly, made nervous by the lateness of the hour and the isolation of the corner office she had been working in.

Biting off a scream, she swallowed hard when she saw the tall, strongly built man standing in the doorway. He was blond, blue eyed, and darkly tanned, wearing faded jeans and a thick knit sweater that clung to the powerful muscles of his shoulders. Her first impression was that he looked like a California surfer who had just walked off the beach. At second glance she realized her mistake. The lines of his face were controlled, strong, almost harsh, and the sharp intelligence of his eyes had little in common with the carefree gaze of a typical surfer.

"Who are you?" he asked, his voice cool but polite. "What are you doing here so late?"

She was careful to make her reply sound equally restrained and courteous. "I'm Cathryn Bracken, and I work for the accounting firm of Kingston and Arthur. I'm one of the auditors assigned to certify Consolidated Vision's annual accounts."

His sudden grin added warmth to his dark blue eyes. "That sounds very believable. Even from the rear view you look more like an accountant than a burglar. There's something so aggressively respectable about gray pin-stripes." He held out his hand, still smiling. "I'm Joshua Hunt."

She shook his hand briefly, concealing a tiny start of surprise as she recognized the name of Consolidated Vision's president. Experience had taught her that company presidents came in all shapes and sizes, but Joshua Hunt looked nothing like any other president she had ever met. Only his subtle aura of self-confidence fitted the presidential mold. Truly successful corporate executives all exuded that same sense of controlled power.

She gave him one of her polite, careful smiles. She had learned quite soon after Robert died that smiles create a much more effective barrier than tears. "As you can see, I was just leaving, Mr. Hunt. My partner and I would be happy to discuss the progress of our work with you tomorrow, if you can spare the time."

He narrowed his eyes, and something in the way he looked at her caused an inexplicable wave of heat to burn in her cheeks. The sensation was so unfamiliar that she couldn't identify its cause. "Why are you working so late?" he asked. "Have you come across a problem?"

"No, your financial department keeps excellent records. But this is a busy time of year for accountants, and I need to finish up here as quickly as I can." She smiled again, the impersonal smile that always worked so effectively to keep a business conversation strictly on track.

He ignored the smile. "Have you eaten dinner yet?"

"No. I was planning to grab a sandwich in the motel coffee shop."

"I just flew in from London, and I always try to avoid eating on planes if I can. Will you wait while I pick up some urgent mail and then have dinner with me?"

She hesitated. Then, reminding herself he was a client, she said, "Thank you. I'd like that."

She saw the skepticism in his expression but pretended to be unaware of it. "Hotel restaurants can become very boring after a while," she added, doing her best to look like a woman who could think of nothing more delightful than an unexpected invitation to dinner. "While you're going through your mail, I'll comb my hair and put on some fresh lipstick."

"I'll be right back." His gaze brushed over her mouth, and disconcertingly, she lost a little of her usual poise.

When she went into the ladies' room and unpinned her thick brown hair, she was surprised to find that her hands were shaking. She formed a soft, smooth coil at the nape of her neck, then brushed brown shadow into the crease of her eyelid, to match her big brown eyes, and added pale coral gloss to her lips. There was no reason for her to be on edge. She had accepted several dinner invitations from eligible bachelors in the year since Robert had died, and she had attended more business dinners than she had bothered to count.

One of the first bitter lessons she had learned after they carried Robert's limp body out of the ocean was that grieving young widows attract male attention and sympathy the way open pots of jam attract flies. In the first few traumatic months after the funeral, she had tried to ward off unwanted attention by fleeing from any hint of masculine admiration. She had quickly learned the folly of that tactic. Nowadays, she was wise enough to hide her aching, tormenting grief beneath calm smiles and apparently spontaneous friendliness.

Most men, she had discovered, weren't especially perceptive. If you laughed at their jokes, encouraged them to talk a great deal about themselves, and allowed them to kiss you good night, they rarely noticed that your emotional response hovered at the level of absolute zero. She had found that the more superficially outgoing she appeared, the less likely most men were to offer her consolation for widowhood in the warmth of their beds.

She straightened her skirt and tucked her white ruffled blouse firmly into the waistband, feeling a touch impa-

tient with herself. She was, she realized, leaping to unfounded conclusions. She had no valid reason to suppose
that Joshua Hunt had any personal interest in her. His
manner had contained none of the sexual innuendo she
despised. His invitation was probably no more than a
courtesy extended to a business associate. She had no
reason to feel so defensive, as if the man had somehow
launched an attack on her privacy.

When she came out of the ladies' room, he was waiting patiently in her office, holding a jacket over one arm,
a bunch of letters sticking out of the pocket. As soon as
she appeared in the doorway, he slid off the desk he had
been sitting on.

"There's a place called Hank's Hamburger Heaven a
couple of blocks from here," he said. "I guarantee it sells
the best hamburgers in Connecticut. Would you like to
try it?"

"With a recommendation like that, how could I resist?"

They got into the elevator and sped silently to the
ground floor.

"Mind if we walk?" he asked as a security guard
hurried forward to let them out of the steel-barred doors.

"Not at all. In fact, I'd prefer it. It's a beautiful night,
and I don't get enough exercise when I'm on assignment."

"How long have you been working for Kingston and
Arthur?"

She answered the question without missing a beat.
"Almost a year now."

"I noticed your wedding ring; it's a very unusual de-
sign. How do you and your husband cope with the de-
mands of a two-career marriage?"

"I'm a widow," she said. She was proud of the way
she could speak the words without any betraying tremor.
She had even learned not to change the subject. In the
long run, it always proved quicker and less painful to

tell the story willingly, so that her escort's protective instincts weren't aroused. "My husband was killed in a scuba-diving accident in the Caribbean. He's been dead for almost eighteen months now." She made herself say the words calmly, but she didn't add that he had died on their honeymoon, the day before they were due to fly back to the States. She didn't add that she had had a miscarriage when she was three months pregnant and that her life had effectively stopped at that moment.

"I'm very sorry," he said, a note of real gentleness in his voice. "It's always terrible to lose somebody you love. It must be even more terrible if you lose them so unexpectedly."

"Yes." The pain of Robert's death was a gaping, tearing wound choking off her breath, but she wouldn't let Joshua Hunt see it. If she didn't let anybody know how fiercely she grieved, she could sometimes pretend the grief wasn't real. She spoke again, forcing herself to mouth the lies that would stop his questions. "It was dreadful at first, but I guess I'm over the worst of it now." She searched for a suitable platitude. "Time helps," she said. "And so does my profession."

"Is that why you were working late tonight?"

She resented the perspicacity of his question; she didn't want him to keep probing her pain. "Oh, no," she lied. "I told you, our firm is very busy right now." She struggled for a moment to bring her emotions back under control, forcing her lips to curve into a relaxed smile. "You mentioned that you've just come back from London. Was it a business trip, Mr. Hunt, or were you lucky enough to find time for an early summer vacation?"

Once again she was aware of a disconcerting rippling sensation in the pit of her stomach when he turned to look at her, but all he said was, "It was a business trip, and please call me Joshua." He gestured ahead of him. "Hank's Hamburger Heaven is across the street, at the corner. I'm getting hungrier by the minute. I think I must have forgotten to eat for the past few days." He put his hand under her elbow, his grip firm as he escorted her across the road.

As soon as they reached the entrance to the restaurant, she moved away from him, but she still kept hold of her smile. "It must have been a busy trip if you forgot to eat. Was it something exciting?"

"Yes. I want Consolidated Vision to start making movies geared to the cable TV market, and I was hoping to get some financial backing in London. But I guess cable television was out of favor with the investment bankers last week."

Cathryn murmured a few words to express her interest. She breathed a quiet sigh of relief as a young hostess led them to an empty table and handed over two menus. Joshua Hunt had given her exactly the opening she needed. With any luck she would be able to keep the conversation strictly on his business plans. A company president on the track of a new venture rarely needed much encouragement to discuss his pet project, and a dinner of broiled hamburgers wasn't going to take long to serve and eat. She should be back in her motel room within an hour and then—at last—she could let herself drown in the bittersweet memories hammering at the edge of her consciousness.

The restaurant's service proved exceptionally prompt. She had scarcely finished reading the menu when a waitress came and took their order for two cheeseburgers, one spinach salad, and one baked potato with sour cream. Joshua added a request for a carafe of red wine.

"They only serve three varieties of wine here," he said with a grin. "Red, white, and pink. I've had the red before, and it's not too bad."

"Don't worry, I'm anything but a connoisseur. Robert tried hard to teach me to have a discriminating palate, but I always ended up liking sweet white wines and spurning his favorite cabernets and burgundies. I remember he ordered a bottle of Dom Perignon for our wedding night, but the bubbles gave me hiccups before I finished my first glass!"

Her voice died away, and she looked up, appalled at the personal details she had unwittingly revealed. She was not reassured when she saw that Joshua was examining her with an intense, speculative expression. "Your husband's name was Robert?" he said.

"Yes." Her answer was more curt than she intended it to be, but she was thrown off balance by her own unexpected behavior and couldn't think of anything else to add. Since Robert's death, she had learned to talk about his accident and her own widowhood, but she had never before allowed anyone to share the precious secrets of her brief married life. She was suddenly angry with Joshua Hunt for breaching the protective barriers she'd erected around her memories.

"Here comes our waitress," he said, apparently unaware of her tension. "She made it just in time. I've already demolished the entire basket of breadsticks."

Cathryn struggled to control her irrational anger. She waited until they had both taken a few hungry bites before determinedly bringing the conversation into the channels she wanted it to follow. "I've enjoyed working with your company this week," she said. "I understand your father founded the company thirty years ago, when he was fresh out of college. Now you own seven radio stations and three cable television franchises?"

"Yes, we've expanded rapidly over the past ten years or so, which I believe is necessary for our survival. I don't think the communications field has room for too many small operations. I want to make sure that our company generates enough income to join the ranks of the big-timers. In my opinion, cable television will be a cutthroat business during the next five years."

"How long have you been president, Joshua? Has your father retired from active control of the company?"

There was an infinitesimal pause as he swallowed a mouthful of hamburger. "No. Actually, my father is chairman of the board and very active in company affairs. He married young, and I was born when he was twenty-three. He's only in his late fifties."

"And your mother?"

"She died when I was a teenager."

"I'm sorry."

"It was bad at the time but, as you yourself said, time heals."

Something in his voice made her look up from her spinach salad, but she decided she must have imagined hearing a faint trace of sarcasm. His eyes met hers with utmost frankness, and his smile expressed nothing more than mild friendship. "My father married again last year," he said. "My stepmother is a charming woman."

Again she wondered if she had imagined the peculiar undercurrent that shadowed his words, but this time she didn't bother to meet his eyes. She sipped her wine, suddenly realizing that she was tired to the point of total exhaustion. She put down her fork, giving up the effort to eat the rest of her salad.

"Where are you staying?" Joshua asked. "At the Olde Colonial Motel?"

"Yes." She smiled slightly, the first completely natural smile of the evening. "It's a funny place. It's so determinedly antique, it even has black plastic beams on the ceiling of the bathroom."

He grinned. "At least it's conveniently close to the office."

"True. Speaking of which, I'd better get back to the motel. I have to make an early start tomorrow morning. Jim, my partner, is one of those early morning freaks."

At once Joshua caught the eye of the waitress to ask for the check. "The motel isn't more than three blocks from here," he said. "Would you like me to walk you home?"

"I can call a cab. I don't want to take you out of your way."

"No problem." He took the check from the waitress and handed her a couple of bills. Cathryn noticed that his casual smile had a devastating effect on the young woman.

As they walked out into the night, the air felt cool after the pleasant mugginess of the restaurant. Cathryn shivered, and Joshua immediately dropped his jacket around her shoulders. "Here, I don't need this. The air feels warm after London."

"I'm sure you must be tired after your trip," she said. "Why don't I call a cab so that you can go straight home?"

"I'd prefer to walk. My father's home is quite close to the motel. I told you, you're not taking me out of my way."

"You live with your father?"

"Yes." He must have heard the slight surprise in her question, for he lifted his shoulders in a tiny shrug. "Consolidated has radio stations all over the Midwest, so I travel a great deal. Until my father remarried, it seemed silly to keep up two bachelor households. But recently, I've been thinking I ought to have a place of my own."

It wasn't difficult to interpret a great deal that he had left unspoken. Obviously his stepmother—his "charming" stepmother—was difficult to live with. Cathryn, however, was not interested in Joshua Hunt's personal problems. She was, in fact, thoroughly irritated by the way she had failed to direct the pattern of their conversation. As far as she was concerned, a great deal too much personal information had been exchanged.

She was dismayed when he walked into the lobby with her, waiting while she picked up her key from the reception desk. As soon as she had the key, she turned around, her hand politely outstretched. "Good night, Joshua. Thank you very much for dinner. I enjoyed it."

He ignored her hand just as earlier he had ignored her

smiles. "I'll see you to your room."

She didn't want him to come with her, but decided it wasn't worth making a fuss. The motel only had two floors, and he followed her up the shallow staircase, turning left along the corridor leading to her room. She fitted her key in the lock and then faced him once again. "Well, good night, Joshua. Thanks for the escort service to my door." This time she didn't hold out her hand, keeping it firmly on the doorknob instead. "I'm *really* glad we happened to meet in your office," she added warmly. She had found there were few things as effective as brisk professional enthusiasm for putting an end to unwanted intimacy. "It's always a pleasure to meet the president of the company I'm working with, and it was certainly much nicer sharing dinner with you than eating alone."

His blue eyes darkened with amusement. "Very prettily spoken," he murmured, his voice husky with unexpressed laughter. "I'm sure your colleagues give you top marks for client relations." His lean fingers grazed her cheek lightly, and her skin tingled where he had touched it. She jerked her head away, not liking the effect he was having on her, but he put his hands around her waist and pulled her against him.

The shock of finding herself in his arms made her temporarily immobile. For a moment she felt breathless expectancy as her body quivered with a curious leaping anticipation, then he bent slowly toward her and covered her mouth with his own.

At the very first touch of his lips, the heat of his arms and chest seemed to transfer itself into her veins and race fiercely through her. She closed her eyes, and his kiss deepened with deliberate seductiveness. She was suddenly aware of an urgent, unfamiliar desire to respond. Her pulse began to beat with a feverish rhythm and, for just a few seconds she parted her lips hungrily beneath his.

As soon as she realized what she was doing, she tore herself out of his arms. "No!" She twisted her head sharply, determined to evade his mouth. "Please stop! I don't want this to happen."

She hadn't meant to look at him, but accidentally her eyes locked with his, and for an instant, she could have sworn she read a shock almost as great as her own in the depths of his gaze. Then he blinked his eyes, and when she looked again, there was nothing except a lingering trace of cool amusement. "I only kissed you good night," he said. "It was very pleasant, but hardly earthshaking."

She knew her reaction was totally out of proportion to what had occurred between them. Joshua wasn't the first man to have kissed her since Robert died, and she had learned to handle unwanted kisses with as much skill as she warded off all other unwanted intimacy. "I'm tired," she said, explaining her behavior to herself as much as to Joshua. "It's been a long day. Perhaps I'll see you in the office tomorrow."

"Perhaps." He released her and turned abruptly away. "Thanks for your company at dinner," he said. "I enjoyed it."

He raised his hand in a brief salute and disappeared around the bend. The muffled sound of his footsteps in the corridor had died away before she managed to unlock the door and barricade herself in the dark, lonely privacy of her room.

Chapter Two

THE ANNUAL FINANCIAL statement for Consolidated Vision took longer to prepare than either Cathryn or Jim, her partner, had anticipated. By the middle of Friday afternoon, it was obvious that they would need to return to Connecticut the following week. No amount of hard work during the afternoon was going to finish up the job.

Cathryn grimaced slightly as she pushed a bundle of unfinished calculations into her briefcase. For some reason she didn't relish the prospect of returning to Consolidated for another week's work.

"Jim, do you mind if I leave now?" she asked. "I ought to get back to the city before six if I possibly can."

"Sure, go ahead. You've put in hours of overtime this week already. Are you planning something exciting? Got a heavy date lined up?"

She carefully zipped her briefcase before replying. "My mother and sister are coming for the weekend. They want to do some shopping."

"Your folks are from Valley Forge, aren't they? What happened to all the stores in Pennsylvania?"

"As an old married man, Jim, you ought to know the difference between shopping in Manhattan and shopping in Pennsylvania."

"Sure do. In Manhattan everything costs twice as much, and there's nowhere to park."

She laughed. "I won't try to argue with you! I have to run if I'm going to make the three-thirty train. See you on Monday, Jim."

The train into Manhattan was almost empty. Cathryn pulled a few papers out of her briefcase, but the computerized data jiggled in front of her eyes, a meaningless jumble of gray dots and dashes. She loved her mother and sister, but she wished they weren't coming into town this particular weekend. It had been a rough week, and she could have used a couple of days alone. There was nothing more exhausting, she had found, then pretending to be happy in front of people who cared deeply about your well-being. And she owed it to her family to pretend she was happy.

In the first couple of weeks after Robert's death, Cathryn knew it was only the love and heartfelt sympathy of her family that enabled her to survive.

Her parents and sister had arrived at the hotel in the Caribbean within hours of Robert's accident. Her mother had swept Cathryn into her arms and cradled her as if she were once again a tiny baby, crooning words of reassurance and sympathy as she rocked Cathryn into an exhausted sleep. In those early days it had often seemed to Cathryn that nothing was real except for her own grief and the life-saving support of her mother's arms.

The rest of the family had helped, too. Her younger sister, Beth, had cried all the tears Cathryn seemed unable to produce. And her father, his face gray with unspoken sympathy, had taken care of the details of the funeral, shielding her from officialdom with determined, dignified efficiency.

As the months passed, however, Cathryn had begun to wish her family would be less protective. They loved her so much that they couldn't bear to see her unhappy. They wanted her to relegate her marriage to the past, and they weren't subtle about suggesting that a new man was what she needed most. Her mother often reminded her that she was only twenty-seven and that her life was still ahead of her.

Cathryn began to resent their assumption that Robert ought to be forgotten, that he was nothing more than a tragic interlude, an unfortunate diversion on her road to a wonderful second marriage. How could they care for her so much yet not realize that part of her soul had died with her husband? Offended by their callousness, she kept the fact of her pregnancy from them, hugging it to herself as a last secret link to Robert.

On the day she came out of the hospital after her miscarriage, she asked her boss for a transfer to New York City. She knew she would go crazy if she didn't get away from Philadelphia, the place where she and Robert had once planned to be so happy.

She had been living in Manhattan for over a year now, renting a small corner apartment in a new building on the East Side. She could hear her neighbor's stereo through the living room wall, yet she doubted she would recognize him if they met on the street.

She didn't mind her loneliness in the least. On the contrary, she relished it. Away from the kindly interference of her family, she was free to live as she wanted— wrapped up in her memories of Robert.

And now she had to face her mother and sister for two days, locked in the intimacy of a tiny one-bedroom apartment. The realization kept her preoccupied as she rushed through the local supermarket, picking up a container of milk and a few other essential supplies. It was difficult to prepare for guests when work took you out of town so frequently, and her sister Beth, who was married, had such a domesticated turn of mind. She seemed to think that if a person had empty kitchen cupboards, that person's life couldn't possibly be running smoothly.

I haven't seen them since Easter, and they'll only be here for two nights, Cathryn thought as she hung up her suit and pulled on a pair of twill slacks and a turquoise cotton shirt. She rubbed tinted foundation beneath her eyes to conceal the shadows and stroked blush carefully across her pale cheeks. The intercom buzzed, and the brush slashed a line of vivid peach color almost to her nose. Oh hell, she thought. There's absolutely no reason for me to be this nervous. I don't know what's gotten into me.

She grabbed a tissue and rubbed her cheek quickly while telling the doorman to send her mother and sister up. She had just opened the front door when Beth burst out of the elevator and ran along the corridor, arms outstretched.

"We're here!" she cried, enveloping Cathryn in a breathtaking hug. "And I didn't get lost once! Let me look at you—oh heavens! Why do you always do this to me? I don't know why I love you so much. I swear you look at least an inch taller and five pounds thinner. How come you're so tall, and I never grew past five foot three?"

Cathryn laughingly returned her sister's hug. "I haven't grown since my fifteenth birthday, Beth, and you know it. Besides, I'm only a couple of inches taller than you." She drew her sister into the apartment and turned to give her mother a welcoming kiss. "How are you, Mom? You're looking terrific. It's been too long since our last get-together."

"It certainly has, and it's great to be here. In fact, it's even better than you might imagine. There were moments driving into Manhattan when I thought Beth's new Chevette might disappear into a pothole and never come out again!"

Cathryn laughed. "What potholes? According to city hall, the roads were all fixed last summer. Anyway, come and put your cases in my bedroom. I thought you two could sleep in there and I could take the sofa. It's quite comfortable for one person."

They followed her across the living room and into the small bedroom. "We've almost nothing to unpack," her mother said. "It'll only take us a couple of minutes to get organized. We were hoping to catch up on all the important news over dinner and spend a leisurely day shopping tomorrow, if you don't have any other plans."

"None at all," Cathryn said. "Sounds good to me."

"Leisurely shopping—some hope!" Beth dropped her bag on the floor. "I can see I'd better get an early night. I know what you're like, Mom, when you're on the track of a bargain. And you're almost as bad, Cathy."

"I'm a reformed character since I moved to Manhattan," Cathryn said lightly. "Are you going to unpack right now? We can eat dinner as late as you want."

"Let's eat now," Beth said. "Frankly, I'm starving. It seems like a week since I ate lunch."

Cathryn patted her sister's rounded stomach with an affectionate smile. "I don't know about me getting taller and skinnier, but you sure have gained a few pounds, Beth. What's up? You've always been so careful about your figure."

Beth and her mother exchanged a swift glance, and Cathryn immediately knew what her sister was going to say. *This* was why they had suddenly decided to pay her a visit, she realized. She thrust her hands deep into the pockets of her pants and watched her sister's face suffuse with shy, excited color.

"Ken and I are going to have a baby," Beth said huskily. "Oh, Cathy, we've been trying for three years, and it's finally happened. We're so happy, I'm practically flying! I even enjoy feeling sick in the mornings because the doctor told me that was a good sign of an established pregnancy!"

Somehow—she had no idea how—Cathryn kept her smile firmly in place, although her stomach had plummeted straight to the floor. She waited for a moment to be quite sure her hands had stopped shaking, then she put her arm around her sister's shoulders and gave her a quick, loving squeeze.

"That's wonderful news, Beth, really wonderful. I'm so happy for you both. For you and Ken." She nervously swallowed a gulp of air. "I didn't realize you'd been having trouble trying to start a family."

Again she saw the swift exchange of glances. This time it was her mother who answered. "Well, Beth and Ken didn't like to discuss their problems with you, Cathryn. You sort of seemed to have enough on your plate to worry about." She cleared her throat uncomfortably. "You know, with Robert and all..."

Cathryn felt her smile slipping disastrously and hastily fixed it in place again. "Sure, I understand. When's the baby due, Beth?"

"Before Thanksgiving." Beth turned away, then swung around again, her face lighting up with irrepressible happiness. "Oh, Cathy, I'm so excited, I can hardly wait for the next five months to go by! It's going to be the best holiday season Ken and I have ever had!"

"I'm sure it will be. It'll be wonderful for Mom and Dad, too. I guess they're dying to be grandparents." Cathryn closed her eyes, but not before she caught a revealing glimpse of her mother's rapturous expression.

She gulped in another breath of air and hurried on. "And Ken's parents, too. They must be excited although they already have one grandson, don't they?"

"Yes, but we're hoping for a girl, and so if we're lucky, it'll be their first granddaughter."

"That's terrific. I can't wait to say hi to my niece, although I think I might prefer a nephew. I always enjoyed playing baseball more than dressing dolls." Cathryn's desperate smile finally trickled away, and this time she knew there was no hope of retrieving it. She edged toward the bedroom door, trying to think of some excuse to justify her hasty departure.

"Why don't you two hang a few clothes in the closet while I fix dinner? It won't take me a minute."

"I'll help you in the kitchen," Beth said. "We can chat while we're working."

"No!" She knew she had spoken much too sharply, and she tried again, forcing the approaching tears away for another minute. "Why don't you lie down for a while, Beth? You know car trips make you sick at the best of times, and it must have been difficult driving through all that late afternoon traffic. Everything's ready for dinner. I just have to put a quiche into the oven and slice a few tomatoes for the salad."

Not waiting for her sister's response, she hurried out of the bedroom and into the kitchen, turning the taps full on so that the noise of running water would hide the sound of the sobs racking her body.

Most of her tears were for Robert's baby, which she had lost without ever having a chance to love. But she was aware of a shocking thread of jealousy twisting its way through her self-pity, and she knew that some of her tears were caused by anger. Why should Beth have a loving husband and a baby on the way when she had nothing? It wasn't that she begrudged her sister the happiness of approaching motherhood, but she was suddenly

starkly aware of the emptiness of her own life. Her future
stretched out before her, hollow and purposeless. And
there was no denying the fact that the void was of her
own creation.

She pushed the quiche into the oven, slamming the
door shut as she adjusted the thermostat. For a brief,
frightening moment she actually hated Robert because
he had died and left her alone to cope with the agony of
survival. It wasn't fair that she should hurt so much when
there was nobody left to comfort her.

She felt the light, tentative touch of her mother's hand
on her shoulder. "Cathryn, are you . . . are you all right?"

"Yes, I'm fine, Mom."

"Cathryn . . ." She heard the hesitancy in her mother's
voice. "Ken and your sister have wanted this baby for
such a long time. Please be happy for them."

Cathryn kept her face averted as she reached for a
tissue from the box on the kitchen counter. "I *am* happy,"
she said, forcing out the lie.

There was a strained silence. "You could have children of your own if you wanted them," her mother said
finally. "You're intelligent, you're healthy, you look terrific, and you have a warm heart. You'd make a wonderful mother."

"You seem to have forgotten one important thing. I
have no husband. He's dead. Dead men can't become
fathers, unfortunately. And as far as I know, virgin births
are still beyond the powers of medical science."

Her harsh, angry words fell into another strained silence.

"I'm sorry," her mother said finally. "There are a lot
of things I could point out to you, but I know you think
it's none of my business how you plan your future."

Cathryn threw away the wad of crumpled tissues. Her
tears were all gone, and she was once again in control.
"If Beth's hungry, we'd better hurry up with dinner.
Maybe you could slice the tomatoes. I haven't done them

yet. They're in the fridge, on the bottom shelf. If you'll excuse me, I'd like a few minutes to fix my makeup."

"Oh, Cathy, why do you worry so much about the way you look? Sometimes I think you'd be happier if you'd only cry more often. What does it matter if your mascara's smudged? We're your family—you don't have to pretend for us. If you're unhappy, for heaven's sake tell us."

"There's a sharp knife in the drawer by the stove. It does a good job of slicing vegetables. Excuse me a second, will you?"

She locked herself in the bathroom, trying to erase her mother's words from her memory, and washed every last trace of tears from her blotched skin. Then she began the job of transformation, starting with tinted foundation, followed by blush, eye shadow, eye liner, lip gloss, powder, and mascara. She had scarcely used any makeup at all before Robert died, but during the past eighteen months she had learned just how valuable it could be. Looking at herself in the mirror as she brushed on the last stroke of mascara, it was impossible to see any trace of the distraught woman who had wept over the kitchen sink.

When she emerged from the bathroom, Beth and her mother were talking in hushed voices. They stopped as soon as they saw her.

"Heavens, Cathy, what have you done to yourself?" Beth exclaimed, her voice high-pitched and unnatural. "I always did think you looked more like a model than an accountant, and New York City sure has added the final polish."

"How do you like living in Manhattan now that you're settled?" her mother interjected hurriedly. "I don't think I'd ever get used to the pace after so many years in a Pennsylvania suburb. Are you starting to mind all the traveling?"

"No. Actually, I enjoy it." Cathryn carried the steaming quiche and the bowl of mixed salad to a small table set in the corner of the living room. She was grateful to her mother for introducing a painless topic of discussion, and she chattered with determined vivacity about the week she just spent in Connecticut. Cable television was an easy subject to make interesting, and she repeated Joshua Hunt's opinions about the future of the industry, relieved to feel the level of tension dropping as they all traded opinions about recent movies made specially for television. She reflected wryly that she hadn't expected her dinner with Joshua Hunt to prove so useful.

Her thoughts wandered as her mother and sister complimented her on the meal, and she recognized with a faint feeling of shock that Joshua Hunt was the chief reason her week had seemed so exhausting. She had been on tenterhooks ever since Wednesday night, wondering if she would see him again, and as it happened, she needn't have worried. As far as she knew, he hadn't set foot in his office, much less bothered her with requests for another date. Not, of course, that she would have accepted any such invitation.

Her mother helped clear away the dishes and carried a pot of coffee and a chocolate cake into the living room. "Beth wants to indulge in a shopping spree for the baby," she said as Cathryn cut three thin slices of cake. "Where do you recommend we should go?"

"Bloomingdale's, I guess. They always seem to have everything." Cathryn wondered how it was possible to sound so cheerful when her heart felt as though it was being twisted inside out. She dreaded spending an entire day cooing over baby equipment. "I haven't looked, of course, but I bet they stock anything you could possibly want. If you have a yen for a French silk christening gown, tomorrow will be your chance to buy it!"

Her sister smiled. "Bloomingdale's sounds fun, but I don't think our budget has room for French silk. A draftsman's salary doesn't allow for luxuries like that."

"But Ken's a *senior* draftsman now—he just got promoted."

"True. Maybe we could afford a silk baby hat in the smallest size."

The ringing of the phone cut through their laughter. Cathryn picked up the receiver, her voice still tinged with amusement as she said hello.

"I'm glad I found you home. I didn't expect to be so lucky. I thought Friday was the big night out for Manhattan's swinging singles."

"Who is this, please?" she asked, although she knew very well who it was.

"It's Joshua Hunt," he said, and she had the infuriating conviction that they both knew she had recognized his voice.

She reminded herself that he was a client, and forced herself to speak politely. "How are you, Joshua? I hope this call doesn't mean you've run into some problems that affect the financial statements."

"This call has nothing to do with your work for Consolidated," he said crisply. "It's strictly personal. I'd like to ask you to have dinner with me tomorrow night, that's all."

"Thank you very much for the invitation, but I'm sorry, Joshua, I'm afraid I can't accept." She felt an unaccountable flash of regret as she gave the automatic refusal. "My mother and sister are in town for the weekend," she added, ignoring the fact that Beth was flapping her hands wildly to indicate that Cathryn should ignore them in making her plans. "They've driven in from Pennsylvania to do some shopping, and we're going to the theater tomorrow night."

"I see. Well, I can tell from your voice that you're absolutely crushed at having to refuse my invitation. . . . You know what? You sound so miserable that

I think I'd better give you another chance to accept this fabulous free offer. How about dinner on Sunday? Your family will have left by Sunday evening, won't they?"

"Er . . . Sunday?" She was disconcerted by the teasing warmth of his voice. Even over the telephone he was able to create that strange, disturbing sense of intimacy.

"You remember Sunday," he prompted. "It's the day that comes after Saturday and before Monday."

She found that she was smiling. She bit her lip, bringing the smile under control. "Well, yes," she said. "I mean, yes, they're leaving on Sunday afternoon."

"Terrific. I'll drive into the city and pick you up at about five. Jim told me you're going to be working at Consolidated's offices again next week, so you can check into the Olde Colonial Motel immediately after we finish dinner. I'm sure you must be missing those beams on the bathroom ceiling by now."

"Well I don't know, Joshua . . ." She turned away so that she wouldn't have to look at the overeager expressions of her family. Dammit, they knew nothing about Joshua Hunt, nothing at all, yet they were obviously longing for her to accept whatever invitation he was offering. Didn't they care at all what sort of a person he was? Was it enough that he should be an unattached male?

"If you spend Sunday night in the motel, it will save you a dreary train ride at seven o'clock on Monday morning, so why not accept?" Joshua said.

He was right about the train ride, and there was no reason in the world for her to refuse, other than an irrational suspicion that it would be emotionally dangerous to become too friendly with Joshua Hunt. And in reality, why should Joshua seem to threaten her hard-won emotional stability? She had accepted a half-dozen dinner dates in the past few months, and the most dangerous consequence had been the threat of lockjaw from too many hours spent stifling yawns of boredom.

"I'd like to have dinner with you," she said finally. "I'll be ready at five, as you suggested. Do you have my address?"

"Yes. I noted it at the same time I got your phone number."

"How *did* you get my number?"

"I looked it up in the directory," he answered, his voice suspiciously apologetic. "It seemed like the most practical thing to do."

She bit back another faint gurgle of laughter. "I'll see you on Sunday, Joshua."

"I'm counting the hours."

She didn't believe him, of course, but she felt an unusual warmth in her cheeks when she hung up the phone.

Her mother and sister were making a great effort to appear uninterested in hearing anything about the call. Her mother jumped up with a great display of energy. "I'll fix some fresh coffee," she said. "This pot's cold."

Beth leaned back against the firm cushions of the sofa. "Is he nice, Cathy?" she asked softly.

"I hardly know him, but he seems quite pleasant."

"His name's Joshua?"

"Joshua Hunt. He's the president of Consolidated Vision, the company I was talking about during dinner. I'm working on their accounts at the moment."

Beth reached out and touched Cathryn lightly on the arm. "Have fun on your date," she said quietly.

"It's a business dinner, not a date." She wasn't sure why she lied. She ought to have seized the opportunity to convince her sister that she led a riotous social life, but somehow she didn't want to admit that there was anything personal about her feelings for Joshua Hunt.

"Well, you can still enjoy yourself. It's not against the law, you know." Beth dropped her gaze to her lap, obviously embarrassed. "It's not even disloyal to Robert's memory," she added quietly.

Cathryn jumped up from the sofa. "I'll go and see why Mom is taking so long with that coffee," she said brightly.

Beth's sigh of resignation was scarcely audible. "Yes," she said. "That seems like a good idea."

Chapter Three

BY THE TIME her mother and sister left on Sunday afternoon, Cathryn wanted nothing more than to curl up in bed with the covers pulled over her head.

She had been glad to see her mother looking well and she had been glad to see Beth looking so happy, but the strain of appearing enthusiastic while they toured the city's baby-outfitting stores had been enormous. She was exhausted when Beth's dark blue Chevette finally turned the corner at the end of the block.

Back in her apartment, her date with Joshua Hunt loomed threateningly on the horizon, the last straw at the end of a trying weekend. She went to change, angry with herself for having accepted his invitation. In retrospect, she wasn't quite sure how it had happened.

She showered and dressed without paying much attention to what she was doing, still exasperated at having committed herself to a date she didn't want. She zipped up her dress with impatient fingers, glancing briefly in the mirror as she applied makeup with the unthinking skill acquired from eighteen months of practice.

She tossed her mascara wand back into her cosmetic purse, displeased to see that anger was causing her brown eyes to flash with an unusual amber gleam. To top off her list of irritations, her hair refused to twist into its normal neat chignon. Little wisps kept escaping from the thick coil at the nape of her neck. She scowled into the mirror, thoroughly disgruntled by her appearance. She looked like the cover illustration for a bad historical novel, she thought with a touch of wry humor. She only needed to pout a little, and the image would be complete.

With an impatient shrug, Cathryn gave up the effort to tame her recalcitrant hair. She flipped off the bathroom light and walked into her bedroom.

The full-length mirror on the bedroom door gave her another unpleasant surprise. She realized that in rummaging hastily through her closet, she had pulled out her beige silk dress without giving it a second glance. It had looked suitably limp and restrained while resting on the hanger. On her body, however, she saw that it dipped too low in front and swirled around her slender hips with provocative suppleness. The dress, she remembered too late, had been hanging at the back of her closet for the last eighteen months, not worn since a prewedding party with Robert. She couldn't understand why she had unconsciously selected it tonight, when, of all nights, she wanted to look her most professional.

The intercom buzzed just as she was looking for the elegant black dress that was her usual evening standby these days. "Mr. Joshua Hunt," the doorman said.

"Please send him up."

The apartment bell chimed seconds later, and Cathryn banged the louvred doors of the closet shut with unusual force. She hurried into the living room and opened the front door.

For a moment she didn't recognize him. He still had blond hair and a tan, otherwise he seemed to bear no resemblance to the relaxed, teasing man who had invited her to share a meal with him at Hank's Hamburger Heaven. He wore a conservative navy-blue business suit with a crisp white shirt and dark silk tie. As he stepped into her apartment, she could smell the faint, spicy tang of an expensive men's cologne. A tiny ripple of awareness snaked down her spine, and she found that her mouth was inexplicably dry. She tried to think of something to say, but her mind was completely empty, not just of witty remarks, but even of trivial courtesies.

"Hi, Cathryn." He smiled, and immediately the Joshua Hunt of the faded jeans and casual sweater returned. "Gray linen pinstripes didn't do you justice," was all he said, but the warmth of his compliment seemed to reach out and envelop her.

"Thank you." Through her dry throat, the words emerged in a husky murmur. She swallowed hard, moistening her lips nervously. "Would you like a drink?"

"I'd like one very much, but I don't think we have time. The doorman's keeping an eye on my car, but it'll probably be ticketed if we don't get downstairs right away."

"Yes, yes, of course. I'll go get my suitcase. It's all packed."

They rode down to the lobby in silence. Cathryn was too busy worrying about her own jumbled emotions to wonder why Joshua was so quiet. A sleek silver Cadillac Cimarron waited for them outside the apartment building, and she glanced up at him with a tiny smile. Somehow, she knew she would be able to tease him without causing any offense. His feathers, she thought, were not easily ruffled.

"Very dignified," she murmured. "And not at all what I imagined you driving. Last Wednesday I had you pegged as the owner of a Jaguar XJS—or a Thunderbird at the very least."

An answering gleam of humor shone in his eyes as he put her case in the trunk. "Interesting to think how often we judge people by superficial appearances, isn't it? You judged me by my jeans and I judged you by your gray pinstripes, and we both discovered only part of the truth. I'm sure there must be a moral to that story somewhere."

The traffic wasn't particularly heavy this Sunday afternoon, and they quickly left the city behind them. It was pleasant driving through the soft light of the early summer evening, and Cathryn was surprised to find the tensions of the weekend gradually draining from her. Joshua spoke easily about the sailing he had enjoyed the day before, and soon she was swapping reminiscences with him about childhood vacations by the ocean. The Connecticut countryside looked clean and fresh after the dust of the city, and she gave a brief sigh of pleasure.

Joshua glanced toward her, his blue eyes very dark in the shadowed interior of the car.

"I hope that's a sigh of relaxation, not terminal boredom."

"Not boredom," she confirmed. "I love the city, but sometimes it's good to get away."

"Then I'm glad I chose a country restaurant. I've made reservations at a place called the Independence Inn. The food's good, and the setting is attractive at this time of year. Lots of geraniums blooming in hanging baskets, that sort of thing. I think you'll like the atmosphere."

"Independence Inn," she said. "And only a couple of miles away from the Olde Colonial Motel, which is right next to the Royal Heritage Shopping Center. You know, I sometimes wonder if the people around here realize that two hundred years have passed since the end of the Revolutionary War!"

"You ought to know the answer to that by now. A native New Englander *never* commemorates a historical event that took place after eighteen hundred."

She chuckled, surprised when she saw that they were already drawing into the restaurant parking lot. It seemed a very short time since they had left Manhattan. Joshua clicked off the ignition and turned to face her, his expression faintly quizzical. There was a brief moment of silence.

"I have a Corvette as well as this car," he said suddenly. His eyes held hers, not allowing her to turn away, and she felt the same strange ripple of awareness that she had noticed when he arrived at her apartment.

"A Corvette?" she repeated, then her mouth curved into a reluctant smile. "Is it a red one?"

"Of course. With black racing stripes."

"Don't you ever drive it into the city?"

"Oh, yes, occasionally."

"Then why did you decide to pick me up in the Cadillac?"

There was another pause, so brief she wondered if she had imagined it.

"Cadillacs and accountants just seem to fit together naturally."

"I didn't realize I was invited out tonight because I'm an accountant who's working for you," she said, and was immediately appalled by the tartness of her response.

A subtle change in his expression vanished before she could interpret its meaning. "I asked you out because I wanted to have dinner with you," he said. "You're a beautiful and intelligent woman, Cathryn. The fact that you're temporarily working for my company had nothing to do with the invitation."

Even before he finished speaking, she began to fumble

for the handle of the car door, anxious to escape from the mood of intimacy she had somehow created. She was shocked when she realized that for almost the first time since Robert's death, she had spoken without weighing the consequences of her words. Looking back on the conversation they had had during the drive, she was disconcerted to realize how often she had expected Joshua to understand ideas left unspoken and thoughts only half expressed.

When he saw that she didn't intend to answer him, he clicked open the electronic lock on the door, and she was free to get out of the car. He was at her side almost immediately, his hand clasping her elbow with a casual, impersonal touch.

"They serve the most wonderful blueberry pie and homemade vanilla ice cream here," he said as they walked into the restaurant. "So make sure you save room for dessert."

She produced a suitable reply and followed the hostess to their table. The restaurant was as pretty as he had promised, and she told him so as they sat down, making a conscious effort to revert to her usual self-possessed manner.

"I felt sure you'd like it," he said, smiling charmingly as he opened the thick leather-bound menu. "As you can see, they serve a wide variety of dishes. The spinach salad is considered a house specialty, and I had an excellent pepper steak the last time I was here. The sole stuffed with shrimp is always good, too, if you happen to like fish."

He gave her time to read over the menu, then spoke entertainingly about a host of trivial subjects while they waited for a waitress to take their order. Cathryn couldn't understand why his easy conversation was beginning to make her feel so nervous, but the rapport she had felt during the journey seemed to have vanished completely.

A cheerful, middle-aged waitress arrived to take their

order. They both selected the sole for their main course, and Joshua ordered a white wine to accompany the meal— a fruity Rhine wine that was one of her favorites.

At that moment the root cause of her uneasiness suddenly clicked into place with the force of an explosion. Joshua's manners were too perfect, Cathryn realized. Why had he bothered to remember her preferences for sweet white wine? With a flash of incredulity, she realized he was doing to her exactly what she usually did to her dates—humoring them, but keeping them at a distance.

She watched him with new awareness, seeing for the first time that he was deliberately fine-tuning his conversation so that it would be interesting but not too demanding. She responded mechanically to his question about the Broadway show she had seen last night and thought how masterful he was at making the conversation seem intimate when in fact it was almost totally impersonal. She found herself wondering whether his courtesy—like hers—was no more than a mask to conceal far deeper emotions.

She had no time to pursue the thought. Their salads arrived, and as the waitress left their table, she saw Joshua give a start of astonishment.

"Well, this is a surprise," he said, putting down his salad fork. "My father has just arrived with ... my stepmother."

If she hadn't been observing him so closely, she would never have heard the tiny hesitation before he spoke the last two words. Moreover, she knew with a sudden, overwhelming certainty that his astonishment was feigned. He had known all along that his father would be here tonight.

Joshua rose to his feet, smiling broadly as he held out his hand to a tall, thin man with youthful features and thick gray hair.

"Father, what are you two doing here? I could have

sworn you said you were eating at the club."

Mr. Hunt shook his son's hand, keeping one arm around his wife's waist. "Now I know you never listen to a word I say, Josh. I told you on Friday that Danielle and I planned to have dinner here tonight."

Joshua grimaced in apparent self-mockery. Friday, Cathryn thought. That's when he called her and made this date.

"Oh, Lord! You've caught me out," Joshua said. "My attention span seems to have decreased to about twenty seconds since I got back from London. Too many nights without sleep, I guess." He turned and nodded to the breathtakingly beautiful woman leaning on his father's arm. His friendly smile never wavered.

"Hello, Danielle. Are you feeling better tonight?"

"Oh, yes, thank you, Josh." Her voice was soft, husky, and almost unbelievably sexy. "Your father has been looking after me wonderfully all weekend."

"That's good. You're looking . . . well."

Cathryn's sensitivity to other people's feelings had been blunted in the months since Robert's death. But now all her instincts warned her that Joshua was not at ease, although she could read nothing but uncomplicated pleasure in his smile. Perhaps that was it, she thought. Perhaps he was smiling too much. It was a tactic she had used so often during the past eighteen months that she intuitively recognized the same device when it was used by someone else.

"Flu is nothing to fool around with," Mr. Hunt said. "You're not as strong as you think you are, Dannie. You still haven't recovered from . . . what happened a couple of months ago."

Because she had remained seated, Cathryn was the only person who saw Joshua's hands clench into tight fists behind his back, and for a moment she held her breath, wondering if he was going to be able to contain the emotion she sensed building in him.

But there was scarcely a broken beat in the rhythm of the conversation, and when Joshua spoke, his tone was merely polite. "I'm forgetting to make introductions," he said. "Cathryn, I'd like you to meet my father, Nathan Hunt, and my stepmother, Danielle Hunt. This is Cathryn Bracken, who's finishing up the annual audit at Consolidated Vision."

Mr. Hunt's eyes were grayer and less friendly than his son's, but he acknowledged Cathryn warmly. "I met your partner at the beginning of the week," he said. "It's a solid company, Kingston and Arthur, one of the best, in fact. You must be good at your job."

"Thank you. I've found the company to be an excellent employer, and I like my work."

His wife raised a pair of the longest black lashes Cathryn had ever seen, exposing eyes of brilliant cobalt blue. She shook hands with an unexpectedly firm grip. "It's nice to know you, Cathryn," she said. Her bewitching voice gave the ordinary words an almost magical significance. "Are you going to be working at Consolidated for very long?"

"An audit normally takes only a few days, Mrs. Hunt. Because of certain investment plans Consolidated has for next year, my firm has been asked to undertake some special financial studies at the same time. I imagine I'll be here for another week at least."

"Oh, it sounds so complicated! You must be terribly clever." Danielle Hunt's husky voice quivered with admiration. "I'm so in awe of successful career women, particularly a woman *accountant*. I've never yet managed to balance my checking account so that it agrees with the bank's!"

Cathryn gritted her teeth. "Some men have problems with their checking accounts too, you know. It's a myth that women aren't good with numbers."

Everybody seemed to ignore her. Mr. Hunt patted his wife's hand fondly, and Joshua said, "You know how to create a real home, Danielle. That's a skill that's every bit as important as keeping your checkbook balanced. Anybody can learn a profession, but it takes a special sort of woman to make a home."

"Do you think so? Really?" Danielle Hunt's eyes were fixed on Joshua, and her pale cheeks flushed a delicate pink.

"I really think so," he said softly.

Mr. Hunt tucked his wife's hand tightly beneath his arm and gestured toward the table. "Don't let us keep you from your meal, Josh. The food here is too good to waste."

"Won't you join us?" Joshua asked.

"No, thank you. I'm sure you and your charming lady would prefer to be alone."

"That's quite all right," Cathryn began, but Joshua interrupted her.

"Thank you for being so understanding," he said. "This is a rather special date for Cathryn and me."

Mr. Hunt looked at them sharply, his gaze openly speculative. With considerable difficulty Cathryn managed to prevent her mouth from dropping open. She turned slightly to avoid Mr. Hunt's penetrating inspection and was just in time to see all the color drain from Danielle Hunt's cheeks.

Cathryn fixed her eyes on the table, biting her lip fiercely, angry at being made the pawn in some complex family game she didn't understand and didn't want to know about. She tried to remember why she had accepted this date and couldn't come up with a single valid reason.

Mr. and Mrs. Hunt soon went to their own table, and Joshua sat down. Cathryn said nothing. She took a mouthful of salad, then occupied herself by spreading butter on a piece of hot crusty bread. She was furious with Joshua and had no intention of initiating a conversation. Although she wondered briefly why she was so annoyed by such a relatively trivial incident, she pushed the speculation aside. It was a long time since she had felt angry—a long time since she had felt any strong emotion except grief—and she found her usual social skills deserting her.

"I was pleased to have an opportunity to introduce you to my father and his wife," Joshua said.

"Were you? Why?"

He looked momentarily taken aback by the cool directness of her questions, then he grinned. "My father doesn't think much of my taste in women. It was gratifying for once to be discovered with somebody who's beautiful to look at and has impeccable professional qualifications."

"Is that why you brought me here? To make points with your father?"

He frowned. "Of course it isn't. I brought you here because I thought you'd like this particular restaurant."

"But you knew your father and stepmother would be here, too."

He looked so startled by her statement that she began to doubt her interpretation of events. "How could you think that?" he asked finally. "As you heard, my stepmother's been sick with the flu. I scarcely expected her to be out of bed, let alone dining out at a restaurant."

She still wasn't sure she believed him, but the first flush of her anger had died, leaving room for other, more rational, feelings. Perturbed by the intensity and range of emotion he had provoked in her during the course of a single evening, she decided to drop the subject. Joshua wasn't important enough to her to force a confrontation. No man would ever be important to her again. Robert was dead, and that was the only important emotional fact in her life.

"What is it, Cathryn?" he asked softly. "Why do you suddenly look so sad?"

She met his eyes without really looking at him. "My wineglass is empty," she said lightly. "That's enough to make me utterly desolate."

He didn't push for a more honest answer. He poured her a second glass of wine and talked amusingly of a movie they had both seen recently in which the gloom and doom had been so overdrawn as to become comic. From movies, he moved the conversation to books. They discovered they had both just finished reading a book about the experiences of pioneer women on the wagon trains leading to Oregon.

Cathryn was amazed when the blueberry pie and vanilla ice cream arrived for dessert. Time had flown by in a fascinating discussion of the role of women in developing the American frontier. She couldn't remember how long it had been since she had enjoyed such a stimulating exchange of ideas.

They didn't linger over coffee. Joshua escorted her from the restaurant, his arm draped casually around her shoulders when he stopped to say a quick good-bye to his father and stepmother.

Danielle Hunt looked fragile, sweet, and very beautiful. Mr. Hunt merely looked thoughtful, although Cathryn had no idea about what.

It was still early, and she wondered if Joshua would suggest they go someplace else, perhaps to a nightclub where they could dance, but he didn't. He drove straight back to the motel, a journey of less than fifteen minutes. As soon as they left the parking lot, he slipped a casette into the tape deck of the car stereo system.

"I think this is a particularly fine recording of Rachmaninoff's second piano concerto," he said, not bothering to ask if she wanted to hear it.

Cathryn told herself she was glad of the music, glad

to avoid the threat of an intimate conversation. But, in fact, she felt more than a little piqued. She was accustomed to cooling the emotional temperature of her escorts; she wasn't used to having them pointedly ignore her.

Joshua waited as she registered at the reception desk, then followed her upstairs to her room. She developed a slight attack of nerves as they walked upstairs together. The effect of the wine was wearing off, and fully sober, she was particularly anxious to avoid a repeat of the good night kiss Joshua had given her four days previously.

They halted in the corridor outside her room, and she smiled the warm, appreciative smile she always reserved for the conclusion of a date, trying hard not to think about the consequences the last time she had used this particular smile on Joshua.

"Well, good night," she said. "Thank you for a really enjoyable evening, Joshua."

She had worried without cause. Tonight he didn't attempt to tease her; he didn't even look at her. He put down the suitcase he had brought up from the car and shook her hand with a cool, firm grip.

"Good night, Cathryn. I can't remember when I last shared dinner with such a pleasant companion." Just for a moment his mouth relaxed into a grin. "Although I still think you're hopelessly confused about how people behaved a hundred years ago."

She quickly withdrew her hand from his clasp, ignoring the knot of tension somewhere behind her ribcage. For a ridiculous moment she wondered if she actually regretted that he hadn't tried to kiss her. She rejected the idea as absurd. Heaven knew, she loathed the good night kisses her dates usually insisted on giving her. And of course Joshua's embrace on Wednesday had been as unwelcome as all the others.

"Well, good night again," she said, hastily fitting her

key into the lock and keeping her face averted. "Perhaps I'll see you some time during the week."

"Maybe. Although I'll be busy."

Even though she wasn't looking at him, she heard the hesitation in his voice and was humiliated. Did he think she had been asking for another date? She quickly pushed open the door and was startled when he murmured something inaudible under his breath. He reached out to restrain her, the solid barrier of his arm preventing her from walking into her room.

For several seconds neither of them moved, then Joshua slowly twisted her around until they were face to face. His hands were cool against her waist, but her skin began to burn with a strange tingling heat everywhere he touched her. He put his fingers under her chin and tipped her head up toward his. Their eyes locked, and Cathryn swayed toward him, unable to control the reflex action of her body.

"Oh, hell!" he muttered. "I didn't mean to do this, not now." He tightened his arms fiercely as he bent toward her mouth.

His kiss was hard, passionate, and demanding in its urgency. His lips moved restlessly against her and almost before she had time to consider what she was doing, she opened her mouth to the insistent thrust of his tongue.

She felt the immediate answering tension of his body and heard the tiny sound, half groan, half gasp, that escaped from his throat. Her awareness of his sexual arousal was unexpectedly exciting. His crushing embrace flattened her breasts against his chest and forced her legs against the hard muscles of his thighs. The softly draped neckline of her dress gaped open, and his shirt buttons dug into her flesh, creating pressure points that were more pleasure than pain. With sudden absolute conviction she knew she wanted to feel his hands caressing her naked breasts.

Her mind was whirling, spinning in confusion at the realization that she had actually invited this kiss and the even more startling realization that she didn't want it to end. She was floating in a velvet-lined void, removed from all contact with reality. Only Joshua's kiss was real, his body the single source of all feeling and emotion.

At first she hardly registered the sound of people gradually approaching along the corridor. As their voices grew louder, however, they penetrated the haze enveloping her brain, and she suddenly realized precisely what she was doing. She was standing outside a motel room passionately kissing a man who wasn't her husband. A man who wasn't Robert. She shuddered with utter distaste and tore her mouth away from Joshua's.

"Stop!" she said. "For God's sake, stop!" She dashed her hand across her mouth, not wanting even to think about Robert with the taste of Joshua's kiss still on her lips. She jerked herself out of his arms. "Somebody's coming."

At that moment, a middle-aged couple rounded the bend in the corridor and halted outside a room a couple of doors away.

Cathryn tucked a loose strand of hair behind her ear, nervously smoothing her dress and trying to pull it more closely across her breasts. She had a momentary impression that Joshua's eyes were blank with shock—as they had been the other time he'd kissed her. But when the chattering couple finally disappeared into their room and she turned to look at him more closely, Cathryn realized she had once again been mistaken. His eyes glittered with nothing more than a trace of unfulfilled desire, laced with rueful humor.

"I must be losing my touch," he said. "Your bedroom door was wide open, and I was kissing you out here in the corridor. I can't believe it! It's years since I was so gauche."

She managed to keep her smile very cool. "You assume too much, Joshua. It's not that easy to get an invitation into my room, however expert your seduction techniques might be."

The smile faded from his eyes. "No, I'm sure it's not," he said. "I already guessed as much." He turned away, his movement abrupt. "Good night, Cathryn. I guess I'll see you around."

This time she went into her room without waiting to watch him leave.

Chapter Four

WHEN SHE WALKED into the Consolidated Vision office early on Monday morning, Cathryn still hadn't decided how she was going to behave toward Joshua Hunt. She felt jittery and emotionally off balance. For the first time since Robert's death, she was uncertain of how she ought to deal with a man. It was an uncomfortable sensation after eighteen months of total indifference to the male sex, and she was angry with Joshua for penetrating her emotional shield. He had no right to make her so aware of the fact that she was a woman.

Her worries and her anger both proved unnecessary, however, because she saw Joshua only when they were surrounded by other people, and he never attempted to speak to her alone. She didn't have to cope with finding a graceful way to refuse his invitations, because he offered her none. Since she didn't want to pursue their relationship, it was absurd to feel piqued by his lack of interest, and with the skill derived from long practice, she convinced herself that she wouldn't have gone anywhere with Joshua even if he had asked.

It was almost six o'clock on Thursday evening when Jim signed the final page of their audit. He put the completed papers into a manila folder and stretched with exaggerated relief.

"Thank heaven we're finally done," he said, pulling on his jacket and reaching into a cabinet to retrieve his suitcase. "I checked out of the motel this morning, and I'm going to try for the seven-fifteen train back to town. My wife's been complaining that she sees more of the man who delivers the dry cleaning than she does of me."

Cathryn's smile was sympathetic. "Have you had a lot of out-of-town assignments recently?"

"I haven't worked in the city for six months," Jim said with a sigh, pushing a pile of papers into his briefcase. "The constant traveling gets tough, but I guess that's what you have to expect in our line of work. Are you going back to Manhattan tonight?"

"No. I'm planning to stay here until tomorrow morning. But you'd better run, Jim, if you're going to catch the seven-fifteen. Don't worry, I'll make sure everything's squared away in the office before I leave."

"Thanks, Cathryn," he said, dashing for the door. "I hope we'll work together again soon. I've enjoyed having you with me on this project." He hurried down the corridor, the sound of his footsteps soon swallowed up in the thick carpeting.

It took almost half an hour to clear out their office and return all the confidential papers to a special steel cabinet with a combination lock. When she was sure that everything was safely stowed away, she leaned tiredly against the cold metal. After a second or so, she jerked herself upright again. There was no reason for her to hang around any longer. She could go back to the motel and have dinner.

She put on her light-weight linen jacket, wondering

suddenly if Joshua Hunt was still in the building. If he was, it would be good business practice to let him know that the audit was satisfactorily completed. After all, he was the president of the company. If Jim hadn't been in such a rush to catch his train, he would undoubtedly have tried to speak with Joshua before he left. It was her responsibility, she decided, to cover for her partner's neglect of a routine professional courtesy.

Cathryn went to the ladies' room and combed her hair until it was absolutely smooth and free of wisps. Consolidated's offices were efficiently air-conditioned, so despite the humidity outside, she looked cool and unrumpled. She flicked a minute speck of dust from the lapel of her jacket. Her suit was navy-blue linen, and she wore it with a pale blue silk blouse that was elegant but undeniably severe in style. She looked so uncompromisingly efficient, Cathryn decided, that nobody could possibly misinterpret her motives in seeking out Joshua Hunt.

She glanced at her watch. Almost seven-thirty. She was sure he'd gone home hours ago, but there was no harm in taking a quick look into his office on her way back to the motel. If he wasn't there, she would leave a polite note on his desk saying that their official report would be mailed to him next week.

With sudden briskness, she returned to the office for her briefcase and walked quickly down the corridor toward the executive suite. The door to Joshua's outer office was open, and his lamp was on. She tapped lightly on the maple panels and stepped inside quickly, before she could change her mind.

He was sitting at his desk, surrounded by several intimidating mounds of paper. Her first thought was that he looked tired. Her second thought was that he looked unhappy, desperately unhappy, with grim lines of concentration etched into his forehead and around his mouth. She was astonished by the wave of sympathy that swept through her when he looked up from the document he was reading, his eyes blurred by fatigue.

He blinked, focusing with obvious effort. "Cathryn! I didn't hear you come in."

"I did knock," she said, "but you were concentrating hard. You look tired, Joshua," she added without thinking, then immediately cursed herself for making such a personal remark.

"I guess I am, but I can't leave yet." There was a lingering hint of weariness in his smile. "It seems as if I have at least a month's paperwork to catch up on. Sometimes I wonder if the government forms on my desk reproduce themselves while I'm sleeping."

"Of course they do. There's probably a Murphy's Law about it."

He fished around in a pile of yellow papers and extracted a long, densely printed sheet. "This is what I was reading when you came in. It's from the FCC, who need to know—by return mail—how many water coolers we have per person employed, how many steps each employee has to walk in order to reach the water cooler, and how many five-ounce cups of water we estimate each employee drinks per day." He waved the paper in the air. "They want seven copies of this. What do you think they're going to do with them?"

She laughed. "I don't dare tell you. It might make you violent. Surely you don't have to fill out that sort of garbage personally?"

"Of course not. Some poor clerk in personnel wasted her time finding suitable answers. But I have to sign it— all seven copies—and that means I also have to read it."

"Every one of those documents will still be on your desk tomorrow morning," she said softly. "And I'm willing to bet the government won't sue even if you don't sign another single page tonight. It's late, Joshua. Isn't it time you called a halt for the day?"

As she finished speaking, he looked up and caught

her eye. He was smiling, and his expression seemed so openly cheerful that Cathryn decided she must have imagined the bleakness she had seen in his eyes earlier. He still looked tired, but she couldn't see any trace of unhappiness in his rugged features.

"To be honest, I'm looking for an excuse to quit," he said. "It would be real easy to persuade me to shut up shop for the night. Have you come to invite me out to dinner?"

"No!" Her denial was too quick, too vehement, breaking the light mood between them. She swallowed hard, then managed to smile casually.

"I'm sorry, Joshua. I'd love to take you out for a meal, but I have work to do tonight that I really can't put off."

"And you're the young woman who was urging me to quit?"

"I have to be in our Manhattan offices by eight o'clock tomorrow morning," she said defensively. "In fact, I really only came to say good-bye. Jim and I have finished the audit, and we'll be sending you our official report next week."

She had her voice under complete control again and was delighted with the way she sounded: cool, polite, a model of professional dignity. Her self-confidence increasing, she walked over to his desk, holding out her hand. "It's been a pleasure working here," she said crisply. "You have an interesting company, Joshua, and a very friendly staff."

He said nothing. Standing up, he took her outstretched hand in his firm grasp. Cathryn felt an irrational quiver of fear. She hastily snatched back her hand, not allowing herself to wonder why his touch seemed so threatening to her self-control.

"I'll be writing to you next week," she repeated, conquering her momentary breathlessness. "Good-bye, Joshua."

"Good-bye, Cathryn."

She was almost out the door when he spoke again. "Don't go!"

She paused on the threshold but didn't step back into the room. He walked around his desk, his casual stride belying the faint note of urgency she had heard in his command, and perched on a corner of the desk.

"I'm going to spend the weekend at a place called Hampton Creek. It's not far from Newport, Rhode Island. My father owns a cottage right on the beach, and he's not using it this weekend. Would you like to come up there with me?"

She had the instantaneous and uneasy feeling that his invitation was not as casually offered as it seemed. She opened her mouth to refuse him—whatever his motives, she had no interest in spending time alone with Joshua Hunt—but the polite words of refusal didn't come out.

"I'd love to spend the weekend with you," she was astonished to hear herself say. "But there's no way I could get up there, Joshua, unless I flew to Newport."

"No need for you to do that." His voice was totally relaxed, with no undercurrent of any sort, and she thought how ridiculous she had been to suspect his motives for inviting her. Just because she had learned to protect her deep grief by saying one thing and feeling another, there was no reason to assume that everybody else in the world behaved the same way.

"I'll drive into the city on Friday evening and pick you up myself," Joshua said. "Can you be ready by seven? Once we're completely clear of city traffic, the drive shouldn't take more than three hours. Even if we stop for dinner, we'll be at the cottage long before midnight."

She pretended to hesitate, but she wasn't deceiving herself even if she managed to fool Joshua. "Well, thank you," she said, after a tiny pause. "I accept with pleasure. It'll be great to spend some time away from the city."

"I'll have the doorman buzz your apartment when I arrive."

"No need. I'll wait for you down in the lobby, so you won't run into any trouble parking."

"Thanks." His blue eyes met hers with unshadowed friendliness, and she told herself again she had been crazy to imagine some hidden motive behind his invitation. Her wariness about personal relationships was obviously beginning to make her paranoid.

"I'll be there on the dot of seven," he said, smiling with great charm. "I'm already looking forward to the weekend. Let's hope the weather stays fine."

"Yes. At least the forecast is good." She turned away from his dazzling smile and mumbled a quick good-bye, suddenly anxious to escape before he could renew his suggestion about eating dinner together.

Before she was back at the motel, Cathryn already regretted the crazy impulse that had caused her to accept Joshua's invitation. What was she going to do if she found herself alone in an isolated cottage with a man she scarcely knew and then had to spend all weekend fighting off his attempts to force her into his bed? If he refused to take no for an answer, she wasn't physically strong enough to make him change his mind. She must have been suffering from a fit of temporary insanity, she thought. Or an unusual upsurge of hormones. She quickly cut off that particular line of reflection, not wanting to inquire too deeply into what it might mean.

First thing on Friday morning, she telephoned Joshua's office, determined to cancel the date. She reached his secretary, who apologized profusely. Mr. Hunt was in a meeting and couldn't be disturbed. Could she take a message for him?

Cathryn was silent for a long time. "No message," she said finally, and slowly hung up the phone. She wondered if she would actually have cancelled their date even if she had managed to reach Joshua.

She was ready at seven that evening, waiting in the lobby as she had promised. She had dressed in an old pair of jeans and a simple cotton shirt, her long hair tied back in a careless ponytail, in the hope that by making herself look outwardly casual and unconcerned, she could make her inner feelings follow suit. Judging by the fluttering in the pit of her stomach, she hadn't succeeded. However casual she might look, her emotions were being churned up to the point of explosion.

Joshua drew up to the curb promptly at seven. He was wearing jeans more faded than her own and a sports shirt that had been washed to an indiscriminate shade of gray. He made no comment on their similar choice of clothing. In fact, he scarcely glanced at her. He greeted her with perfect politeness and congratulated her teasingly on being punctual.

"A beautiful woman who can tell the time! What a rare treasure!"

She cued her mood from his. "How quaintly old-fashioned you sound," she murmured, handing him her overnight bag. "The complete male chauvinist, in fact."

He put her bag into the trunk of the car. "Them's fighting words, lady," he said, slamming the lid.

She gave him a small, careful smile to indicate that he shouldn't take her protest seriously. When she had married Robert, she had considered herself a feminist. Since his death, she hadn't bothered to defend her view that society often treated women as second-class citizens. She didn't want any emotion, not even intellectual anger, to disturb the calm neutrality of her relationships with men, so she was surprised to detect a faint note of belligerence in her voice when she spoke again. "Most women I know are extremely punctual, at least as punctual as the men I know."

He grinned. "I'm too smart to get started on *that* particular argument," he said, ushering her into the passenger seat.

And she certainly had no intention of pursuing it. She watched as he eased the car into oncoming traffic. "I see you brought your Corvette this time, not the Cimarron," she said, only too willing to change the subject.

"Yes. I decided Cadillacs and casual weekends by the sea didn't go well together."

She wondered what he meant by a casual weekend. "It's—um—it's a nice car," she said quickly. "I've never driven in one before."

As they drove out of the city, he explained its advantages, and Cathryn contributed a few remarks about a Triumph racing car her brother-in-law had once owned.

Similar polite conversation lasted almost the entire journey. Joshua was a model host—the sort of escort Cathryn usually craved on her occasional evenings out. He kept the tape deck carefully stacked, and the constant soft background music would have covered any awkward period of silence. But there were no awkward silences, because Joshua didn't allow the conversation to falter, not even for a minute. He pointed out places of interest, commented on the favorable weather forecast, and generally made himself thoroughly agreeable. They stopped for dinner at a small seafood restaurant.

"The food's good here," he promised her.

He had understated the case, Cathryn discovered. The food and the service were both excellent.

But the delicious meal did nothing to appease her mounting case of flaming bad temper. Joshua resumed his travelogue once dinner was over, and listening to his charming, witty comments, she found herself growing angrier with every mile that passed.

"We're nearly there," he said when they finally turned off the highway onto a narrow road. His voice became solicitous. "I hope you're not feeling too tired."

"I'm feeling fine," she said curtly.

"That's good. This can seem like a long drive at the end of a busy week."

She squirmed in her seat, suddenly unable to control her rage. Because his tactics were so similar to her own on dates with men, she knew exactly what he was doing to her. Besides, he had done this to her at least once before, when he had taken her to dinner at the Independence Inn.

"For goodness' sake, stop humoring me!" she ordered in a low, tense voice. "Joshua, please, I'm not a small child who needs to be amused during a boring journey."

He kept his eyes on the road. "I'm not humoring you, Cathryn. I can't imagine what you mean."

"I'm asking you not to patronize me. If you're tired, if it's been a tough week, if you have problems on your mind, please say so. For heaven's sake, don't feel obligated to entertain me. I'm not so empty-headed that I'm going to fall to pieces if there's five minutes of silence in the car."

There was a momentary pause. "I'm sorry," he said finally. "I've developed a bad habit recently of talking about trivialities when my mind is wrestling with another problem. Most people aren't as observant as you are, so they don't notice what I'm doing."

"I'm not sure how observant I am," she admitted quietly. "But I recognized one of my own tricks."

"Tricks?"

She turned her head and stared out into the darkness. "When Robert . . . when my husband died, I discovered people wouldn't let me be alone, and they wouldn't let me be silent. Unless I was talking, everyone seemed to assume I was brooding. Better yet, they wanted to see me laughing." She shrugged. "So I got very good at laughing when I felt much more like crying. I also learned to talk about one thing and think about another. And that's what you've been doing, Joshua, ever since we left Manhattan."

He was silent as he shifted into park, then he turned to face her. "I apologize again," he said. There was a tiny pause before he continued. "My father and I have different opinions on the way our business should be developed, and our strategy differences are on my mind at the moment. It's tough to have the title of president without actually having the power to make your decisions stick."

"I'm sure it must be."

"Let's make a deal. During this weekend, if you want to wander off somewhere and be by yourself, just let me know. I won't try to stop you from being alone, and I won't feel obligated to keep a polite conversation going simply because you're my guest. How does that sound?"

"It sounds fabulous." Her words emerged with unexpected huskiness, and she quickly opened the car door. Clearing her throat nervously, she said, "The smell of the sea is very strong. Is it close by?"

"Twenty yards away. The cottage is separated from the beach only by this parking space and a small area of grass."

He unlocked the trunk. "Grab your suitcase, and I'll carry our box of provisions into the kitchen. I think you'll be impressed with the layout of the cottage. My father designed it himself about five years ago, and he did a terrific job. I've often told him I think he's a frustrated architect at heart."

The cottage was as attractive as Joshua had claimed. It was fairly small, but luxuriously equipped with obvious attention to ease of maintenance. On the ground floor there was a utility room, a modern kitchen, and a comfortable living room. The living room had a Mexican quarry-tile floor, high cathedral ceiling, and bare white walls. The dining table was glass, and it was ringed by four black leather and chrome chairs. The sofa and armchairs were covered in a brightly patterned cotton print: yellow and white daisies dancing across a vivid green background. Upstairs there were two bedrooms, each furnished with a queen-size bed and a row of built-in closets, and each connecting to a small private bathroom. In one bedroom the bedspread and drapes were bright yellow. In the other, they were bright green.

Cathryn was impressed and said so.

"My stepmother did all the decorating," Joshua told her. "The cottage was just a dull old bachelor retreat until she worked her magic."

"Highly effective magic," Cathryn commented.

"Yes," he said, his voice curiously lacking in expression. "My stepmother is a very talented woman."

He turned away, making a halfhearted effort to smother a yawn. "You know, that bed looks very inviting," he said, dropping his small overnight bag onto the bright green spread. "Would you mind if we called it a night and plan to make an early start tomorrow morning?"

"I wouldn't mind at all. I'm looking forward to sleeping with my windows open and breathing in some of that good sea air." She picked up her small suitcase and walked toward the door, smiling brightly. "Good night, Joshua. I'll see you tomorrow morning."

He returned her smile with one equally as bright. "Sleep well, Cathryn. Get up whenever you feel like it. There's no rush."

Her smile faded as soon as she was out of his sight, but she had taken a shower and was stretching out across the fresh sheets of the big yellow bed before she realized what was bothering her. She had learned as a young woman that when a man invited her away for the weekend, he expected to end up in her bed. Joshua was an attractive virile man and yet he hadn't even suggested that she might want to share his bed. What was wrong with her? Had she begun to look old and faded since Robert died, no longer attractive to men?

She rolled over onto her stomach, pulling the sheet up under her arms. It didn't matter in the slightest if she wasn't pretty; of course it didn't. The question of how she looked was completely irrelevant to her life nowadays, because she no longer had any desire to be attractive to men. And she *especially* didn't want Joshua Hunt to find her attractive. He wasn't her type at all. She had never liked men with blond hair and bulging muscles. She had found that the larger a man's biceps, the smaller his brains and the more inflated his ego.

It was somehow reassuring to remember that she wasn't attracted to Joshua Hunt. She reached out and flipped off the bedside light, feeling unexpectedly sleepy.

When she woke up the next morning, she realized that for the first time in eighteen months she had fallen asleep without thinking of Robert. She wasn't sure whether to be glad or sorry.

When she came downstairs, Joshua had already prepared a simple breakfast of coffee and cereal. The sun was shining out of a cloudless blue sky, the coffee smelled wonderful, and Cathryn suddenly felt sure that the weekend would be fun. She sipped her coffee in silence, glad to find that Joshua didn't feel a need to be witty at the breakfast table. Early morning cheerfulness definitely wasn't her thing.

The pleasant indolence she felt was fiercely jolted when Joshua suggested they go sailing. She put her coffee cup back on its saucer, where it rattled before coming to rest, and she saw that her hands had started to shake. She dropped them into her lap and the shaking stopped, but for a moment or two she couldn't speak.

How dumb she had been. Joshua had already told her how much he enjoyed sailing. The America's Cup Challenge races were held off Newport, Rhode Island, and the coast was dotted with boatyards and marinas. She ought to have realized a sailing trip would be on their weekend agenda, but somehow she had never thought at all about what she and Joshua would do during the two days they were together. She had been too busy reassuring herself that they wouldn't spend their nights in the same bed to think about where and how they would spend their days.

She swallowed hard, trying to find the courage to say she would go with him. She hadn't been sailing since her last fatal excursion with Robert, and she knew that she still wasn't ready emotionally to tackle a day's sailing. Rationally, however, she knew it was time she laid her lingering fear of the ocean to rest.

"Cathryn?" Joshua repeated, obviously mystified by her long silence. "Is there some problem? You mentioned once that you'd learned to sail as a teenager. I thought you'd like to take the boat out for a couple of hours this morning. But we don't have to go if you'd prefer to do something else."

With a phenomenal effort of will she thrust the images of Robert and the treacherous blue Caribbean out of her mind.

"Yes, I'd like to come with you," she said, wondering if he heard the tremble in her voice. She gripped the edge of the table and forced herself to look him squarely in the eye. "What sort of boat do you have, Joshua?"

"An O'Day Eclipse. I've been quite pleased with it. I used to have a Tanzer twenty-two-foot racer, then I won a couple of competitions and I told myself I deserved a bigger boat."

"Do you race a lot?"

"A fair bit. But having a weekend cottage near Newport helps keep my ego under control. Compared to most of the people sailing around these waters, I'm a rank amateur. I'm just good enough to be allowed to sit at the end of the dock and listen silently while the real sailors talk." He smiled, then stood up and carried their dishes to the sink. "I'm all set to leave whenever you're ready."

The marina where he kept the boat was less than two

miles away, and to Cathryn's mind, they arrived there far too soon. She noticed nothing at all about the layout of the boatyard, and her stomach knotted with fear as she stepped onto the deck. For the first few minutes, she responded to Joshua's orders in a state of almost catatonic numbness. To her surprise, however, she found that her old skills soon returned. She struggled to conceal her fear from Joshua as she responded to his rapid instructions and, in her effort to appear unafraid, discovered that the worst of her fear had truly vanished.

Once they were away from the dock, she could see that Joshua was an experienced sailor, and her needle-sharp tension dissipated further. They sailed out of the harbor into the open sea with the sun on their faces and the cool wind blowing steadily at their backs.

They reefed the sail and continued to run before the wind. The water was calm, and after a while there was little for Cathryn to do.

"This is the life," Joshua remarked with a contended sigh. He flipped open a can of Coke. "Here, do you want one?"

She drank thirstily, glancing back toward shore. "We can't see the cottage," she said.

"No, we're quite a decent way out." Joshua chugged down the rest of his soda, then returned the empty can to the cooler. "I'd like to take you around the point and into the next bay. Do you mind if we stay out until later in the afternoon? There's food in the cooler if we get hungry."

"I don't mind how long we stay out," she lied. "Nobody's waiting for us, and nothing's burning in the oven."

She adjusted her weight carefully and leaned back against the side of the boat. She closed her eyes and felt the sun's warm rays on her face, the breeze tossing her hair forward into her eyes. The knot of tension in her stomach loosened a little more, and she began to think that perhaps—at last—she was overcoming the fear of the ocean that had haunted her for the past year and a half.

She had no idea how long she sat there, her eyes closed, lost in bittersweet memories of the past. Suddenly she realized that the temperature had dropped. The sun no longer burned against her eyelids, and the smooth, forward progress of the boat had changed into a tossing, roiling motion. She looked up at the sky and saw that the sun had disappeared completely behind an ominous silvery-black cloud. A strong, puffy wind had picked up, all the more hazardous because it was changing direction erratically and rapidly.

Joshua turned to her. "Take the tiller," he said. "Head up into the wind. I'm going to drop the mainsail."

She managed to take the three steps necessary to change places with Joshua at the helm. He held out a life jacket. "Put it on," he said.

She stretched out and accepted the jacket, but she couldn't remember how to put it on. It was unfair of Joshua to expect her to do two things at once. How could she put on the jacket *and* hold the tiller? She let the jacket slide to the deck, her last conscious action before her brain and body both froze with panic. She clutched the tiller with a force that turned her knuckles white, heaving it desperately from side to side in reaction to every sway of the boat.

"Put on your life jacket, dammit!" Joshua called. "And head *into* the wind! I have to haul in the sails!"

She was drenched with spray, and it seemed to her terrified eyes that the white-capped waves broke against the hull with battering force. The boat lurched sickeningly to starboard, and she jerked reflexively on the tiller.

"Leave the tiller free, for God's sake!" Joshua yelled. "Dammit, Cathy, what's wrong with you? Are you trying to capsize us?"

She scarcely heard him. She no longer saw the gray

Atlantic. Instead, the brilliant blue of the Caribbean appeared in front of her eyes. With horrifying clarity she saw the tropical thunderstorm that had claimed Robert's life. In her imagination, she saw the aquamarine waters of the Caribbean darken to indigo. Then, as if it were happening all over again, she saw the boat she was in command of being tossed off course by the storm. Robert and the man he was diving with were left underwater, hundreds of feet away from the boat.

"No! He can't be hurt! I won't let him be hurt! Oh, my God! Robert!"

She had forgotten she was sailing off the Rhode Island coast. She had forgotten all about Joshua Hunt, but he must have heard her anguished words, for he suddenly shouted her name so loudly that it cut into her nightmarish memories. She looked up, blinking her eyes rapidly, and saw him leap across the boat toward her, miraculously avoiding ropes and rigging. She was too disoriented to move, and he grabbed her arms with bruising power, forcibly loosening them from the tiller.

"I'll take that. Go check the pump," he ordered tersely.

She went below, following his order numbly. She saw that the pump was operating efficiently, then realized that she had sloshed through a couple of inches of water in order to reach it. She found a mop and began to clean up the cabin's soaking wet carpets. Her shoulders were aching from the effort when Joshua took the mop from her hand and rested it in the pail. He put his hands around her waist, gently pulling her toward him.

For a long time they just stood together while he held her in his arms, not saying anything. Then he cupped her face in his hands, brushing his thumbs softly across her high cheekbones.

"The sun's shining again," he said finally. "The storm's all over."

"Yes." She gave a tiny gasp. "Yes, I can see it is."

"What happened, Cathy?"

She deliberately misunderstood his question. "You must know what happened...the wind came up. That was a localized squall."

"Why were you so frightened?" His voice remained gentle, not at all accusatory.

"I guess...because of the storm."

"Cathy, you told me once that you've been sailing since you were fourteen, and I've sailed these waters since I was nine or ten. You should have known we weren't in any danger. I doubt if the wind reached more than sixteen knots, and the currents here aren't dangerously strong."

"I know."

"Please tell me what happened to you, Cathy. You seemed to be paralyzed with fear."

His hands were warm against her chilled skin. When she suddenly started shaking, he took off their life jackets and encircled her in his embrace. She felt the cool dampness of his jeans against her legs and the heat of his body against her ribcage, and gradually her convulsive shuddering ended.

He waited until she was completely still in his arms, then he put his forefinger under her chin and tilted up her face. "Tell me how Robert died," he said softly.

Chapter Five

SHE LOOKED INTO his eyes and felt her entire body grow rigid with rejection. "No," she cried. "No, I don't want to talk about it! I don't want to remember!"

He held her close to his warmth, not allowing the shivering to start again. "You may not want to remember, but you can't forget," he said. "Tell me what happened, Cathy. It will help, I promise."

The bitterness of her loss was a physical lump of pain lodged somewhere in her stomach. The pain swelled until it filled her lungs and her throat and burst out in a torrent of angry words. For the first time since Robert's death, she allowed herself to express all the hurt and fury she had tried to keep hidden deep inside her soul.

"It was the last day of our honeymoon," she said. "We went sailing. Robert had done some scuba diving when he was a teenager, so he was fairly experienced.

I wasn't, so he made his dive with a local man he'd met at the hotel. A storm came up—it hadn't been forecast, and it was only severe in our area. The anchor didn't hold the boat. The investigators said afterward that the chain was faulty. While I was trying to get the boat under control, Robert was stung by a Portuguese man o'war. He didn't know it, but he was allergic to its venom, like some people are allergic to bee stings."

Her knees were shaking so much that she was sure she couldn't have remained standing if Joshua's arms hadn't been holding her upright. "That's all there is to tell. I don't want to talk about it anymore."

"You need to tell somebody the whole story," he said quietly. "And I'm here to listen, Cathy."

"I don't need you to listen," she said. "Just go away. I don't want your sympathy. I don't need sympathy." She closed her eyes, but he didn't go away, and his arms still circled her waist.

"Please," he said softly. "Tell me what happened next."

She licked her lips. They tasted salty. She touched her cheeks and was amazed to find that she was crying. She stared incomprehendingly at her wet fingers. "I never cry," she said.

Joshua traced the path of a tear all the way down her cheek as far as her chin, but he didn't contradict her. "Cathy, what happened after the man o'war attacked Robert?"

She had no idea why she continued with her story, but the words suddenly poured out of her in a hurried, flat monotone. "He went into an immediate convulsive reaction and his throat closed up, so he couldn't breathe properly. The other diver brought him to the surface, but they were forty feet under water and they had to surface slowly. The other guy...I guess he wasn't that strong a swimmer, and the storm had driven the boat a long way from where they were diving."

Her voice faded, but this time Joshua made no comment and eventually she spoke again, her breathing harsh and her words clipped. "Robert was dead by the time they reached me."

"What difference would it have made if the boat had been closer, Cathy?"

"None at all!" Angrily, she jerked herself out of his grasp, thrusting him violently away when he tried to touch her. "It wouldn't have made any difference if I could have kept the boat at anchor, I know it wouldn't! The doctor said it would have made no difference!"

He pulled her back into his arms as roughly as she had jerked out of them, clamping her wrists to her sides when she tried to push herself away again. "Then why are you so angry with yourself?" he demanded. "Why do you feel so guilty if it wasn't your fault?"

If he hadn't been holding her wrists, she would have hit him. "I don't feel guilty!" she screamed. "And it wasn't my fault! I didn't kill him. I didn't!" Her silent tears now changed into great wrenching sobs that tore at her lungs and threatened to rip open her heart.

"Of course you didn't kill him," Joshua said quietly. He released his grip on her wrists and ran his hands rhythmically along her spine, rubbing warmth and comfort into her chilled body. "And it's good you don't feel guilty, because you have absolutely nothing in the world to feel guilty about. It would have made no difference if the boat had been closer, Cathy. You know it wouldn't."

His comforting words fell into a pool of silence that seemed to grow deeper and more fraught with tension by the second. She felt her face contort into an agonized, uncontrollable grimace of grief. "It *would* have changed things," she whispered. "It's my fault he died."

Joshua's eyes darkened slightly, but his face showed no other trace of emotion. With the back of his hand, he brushed her hair away from her forehead. "Why is it your fault?"

She couldn't meet his eyes. She didn't want to look at him when she finally admitted her guilt—the dark secret she had kept hidden from everybody, even from her mother. "There was a fully stocked first-aid kit on board. If I'd kept the boat where it should have been, we could have given Robert a shot of adrenaline. It would probably have saved his life. But I couldn't control the boat. After all those years of sailing, I couldn't even keep it close to where he was diving."

He cupped her face in his hands and pulled her head around so that she was forced to meet his eyes. "Cathy, after all those years of sailing, you know there was nothing you could have done. A tropical storm blew up, and your anchor chain broke. That's an act of fate, not something you have to blame yourself for. Your husband went into acute allergic shock forty feet under water. He'd probably stopped breathing several minutes before he and his diving buddy hit the surface. You're not guilty of some crime because you couldn't control the weather. It would be just as logical to say Robert was negligent because he didn't know he was allergic to the venom of a Portuguese man o'war. Dammit, Cathy, there are some accidents you can't guard against if you're ever going to get out of bed in the morning."

She felt her tears stream freely down her cheeks. "Why did he have to die, Joshua? He was so young and strong . . ."

"You know I can't answer that question; nobody can. Some people believe God has a plan that will eventually make sense of all the injustices. If you're not religious, I guess you just have to muddle through as best you can. But in either case, blaming yourself is the least helpful thing to do. I'm sure Robert wouldn't blame you."

She stared out over the ocean, gazing into the distance without consciously registering the shimmer of the horizon, where the blue sky met the white-flecked sea. "We loved each other so much," she said. "We were so good together."

"I know." Joshua squeezed her tight for a moment, and she allowed her head to rest against the comforting hardness of his chest. She could feel the warmth of his skin through his damp cotton shirt, and it felt strangely soothing against her cheek. She sighed, aware of an inner peacefulness that had long eluded her.

Neither of them spoke for several minutes, then Joshua held her at arm's length. "Hey, did you hear that noise?" he asked.

She blinked. "No. What noise?"

"My stomach growling. How could you have missed it? It sounded like the approaching tanks of the Eighth Army."

She was astonished to feel her mouth curve into a smile. "I guess my mind was on higher things."

"Lady, there is absolutely *nothing* higher than a man's stomach."

She laughed. Unbelievably, she laughed. She punched Joshua lightly, then moved out of his arms and sat down near the prow. "It's nearly two o'clock," she said, glancing at her watch. "No wonder your stomach's protesting. Is there anything good to eat in that cooler?"

"Sure is. You can rely on me, ma'am, to provide a gourmet feast." He lifted the lid with a flourish. "Now, what do we have here? Designer napkins with a picture of a yacht in each corner—no tacky bargain brands for us. Cheese and crackers, cellophane-wrapped. Two ham sandwiches. A package of potato chips and a box of pretzels. Not to mention a bunch of grapes and four cans of beer."

"Potato chips *and* pretzels?" she murmured. "I see

you believe in peak nutrition as well as gourmet food."

"I will ignore that snide comment," he said, arranging the various packages on the lid of the cooler, then using it as a tray to carry the food over to where she was sitting. He placed the lid carefully between the two of them, then leaned forward to reach for a beer.

As he stretched across her, she put her hand on his arm, and he looked up, his eyes a brilliant clear blue in the afternoon sunlight.

There was a long moment of silence between them. "Thank you, Josh," she said finally.

"You're welcome." He touched her cheek very gently, and she turned her face to press a fleeting kiss into the palm of his hand.

He didn't remove his hand, and the silence grew until it seemed to become a throbbing, tangible presence between them. Slowly, Joshua twisted his fingers through her hair, pulling her toward him at the same time that he pushed aside the makeshift tray. He hesitated for a fraction of a second, his lips only a breath away from hers, then he closed his eyes and bent to kiss her.

His lips were cool against her mouth, and she could taste sea spray on his skin. He made no attempt to deepen the kiss, yet she was aware of a warm spiral of desire unfurling inside her. Instinctively she moved her lips against his, but even as she did so, he drew sharply away. He stood up and walked around her to the cooler, returning with two cans of beer in his hands and a charming smile on his face.

"My stomach has just switched over from passive rumbling to active protest," he said, unwrapping a ham sandwich. "If you want your fair share of this gourmet feast, you'd better eat fast."

She followed his lead, acting as if the brief kiss had never happened. The rest of the afternoon passed quickly, filled with the routine chores of sailing. By the time they

arrived back at the marina, she was almost convinced
that she had imagined the quick flare of guilt she had
seen in Joshua's eyes just before he kissed her. And she
was absolutely convinced that she didn't feel a moment
of regret that their brief embrace had been over so soon.

Back at the cottage, she showered and washed the
tangles out of her hair, then wrapped a towel around
herself and sat down in front of the dressing table to blow
it dry. Because her hair was thick and heavy as well as
long, it took some time to dry completely. She watched
the shiny strands curl around her brush and thought how
strange it was that today she had revealed her most intimate secrets to a man she scarcely knew. Stranger yet,
she felt few regrets. In many ways, she decided, she felt
considerably happier than she had for months.

With a sudden upsurge of well-being, she tossed the
towel onto the bed and rummaged around in her bag for
some clean clothes. She pulled out a fragile peach-col-
ored bra and matching panties, then completed her outfit
with a pair of white cotton slacks and a thin peach sweater.
She hesitated for a minute in front of the mirror, wondering whether she should apply her usual elaborate
makeup. In the end, she merely brushed gloss over her
lips and sprayed perfume around her neck and shoulders
before running downstairs to the kitchen.

Joshua was already there, revealing a distinct lack of
organization as he haphazardly opened and shut cupboards. He had changed into faded jeans and a navy blue
cotton knit shirt, and the dark colors highlighted his thick
gold hair and glowing bronze skin. Cathryn felt a piercing
quiver of purely physical awareness shoot through her,
and she smiled a touch wryly. She had to admit that
Joshua Hunt was an amazingly sexy man.

"I'm here," she said. "Can I help?"

He pulled his head out of a cupboard and triumphantly

waved a can of chili powder. "Found it!" His eyes roamed over her in explicit appraisal, then he whistled appreciatively. "You look terrific. The sun has colored your cheeks, and it suits you."

"Thanks." She was annoyed that she sounded so breathless, and she gestured to the piles of food arrayed on the counter. "That looks like an interesting collection of ingredients. What have you decided to make for dinner?"

He gave a faint grin. "I was making a halfhearted attempt at tacos, but I don't think I've gotten very far. I already know you're loaded with brains and beauty. Do you, by any miracle, also know how to cook?"

"You're in luck. I'd say tacos are just about within my capability."

He gave an exaggerated sigh of relief. "That's fabulous news. Until you came down, I was beginning to think it would be TV dinners or nothing. Most of the women I meet nowadays seem to have decided that cooking is definitely a man's job."

"And you don't think it is?"

His eyes twinkled. "There's no need to sound so aggressive, Cathryn. In principle, I accept that since both men and women need to eat, both of them should be able to cook. However, I seem to be totally lacking in natural talent. I regularly burn TV dinners to charcoal, and when I make canned soup, it turns out lumpy."

"Nobody can make lumpy canned soup."

"Believe me, I can. If you ask me nicely, I'll even teach you how to do it."

She smiled. "Why don't you take cooking lessons, for heaven's sake?"

"I'm holding out until I get married. I'm afraid that if I learn to cook while I'm still a bachelor, I'll never know if my wife has married me for my lovable personality or just for my cooking. After all, a man wants to be appreciated for something more than his flair with the frying pan."

"I'm sure he does." She opened a can of tomato paste, aware that her heart was beating unusually fast against her ribcage. "Would it compromise your principles too much if I asked you to set the table?"

He grinned lazily as he strolled toward the door. "I'll do it right away. I'll open the wine, too. Once I'm safely away from the kitchen stove, I'm amazingly domesticated."

Dinner was a relaxed and enjoyable meal. Joshua was extravagant in his praise of her tacos, and conversation flowed easily between them. It was almost ten o'clock when he volunteered to clear the dishes while she made coffee. When the kitchen was tidy, he carried the coffee into the living room and sat down in front of the fireplace, pulling a fat cushion off the sofa for Cathryn to sit on. As she settled beside him, he gestured to the empty grate.

"Sometimes, even at this time of year, it's cold enough at night to light a fire."

"That must be nice." She cradled her coffee cup on her stomach and nestled more deeply into the cushion. It was a long time since she had last felt so relaxed. "There's something almost sensuous about a hot summer's day followed by a cool night, don't you think?"

"I guess so. I've never really thought about it."

His words sounded slightly jerky, but she was too somnolent to care. She had the vague impression that Joshua was restless, on edge, but she couldn't pin her feeling down, and she lacked the energy to define her impression more clearly. He got up and selected a tape, then stood in front of the fireplace instead of returning to her side.

The lush sounds of Tchaikovsky's first piano concerto filled the room. She found herself thinking that he always used music when he wanted to block out real communication between them, but the significance of the thought left her mind as she drifted into a pleasant state somewhere between waking and sleeping.

She was jerked abruptly back into wakefulness by the sound of Joshua's voice. It sounded harsh against the lyrical romanticism of the piano concerto. "Do you think you could ever fall in love again?" he asked. "Really in love, I mean. The way you were with Robert?"

She was stunned by his question and obscurely hurt by his curt tone. Drawing in a sharp breath, she pulled herself ramrod straight against the cushions. "No," she said vehemently. "Of course not. I could never, ever love anybody the way I loved Robert."

He kicked at a driftwood log that rested in the grate, keeping his back toward her. "What makes you so sure, Cathy? Maybe later, a few months from now, you'll meet somebody special and find that your feelings have changed completely."

She was angry that he should think her love for Robert was so superficial that it would fade away as soon as she met a prospective husband. "You're quite wrong," she said coldly. "The sort of feelings Robert and I had for each other come only once in a lifetime. He was the best friend I ever had, as well as my lover. I could never love anybody that way again."

"I can understand that," he said. She was secretly a little surprised that he didn't dispute her words, but of course she didn't admit as much to him. He gave the driftwood one last kick, then came and knelt beside the low table, pouring them both a fresh cup of coffee.

"Have you considered the possibility of getting married again?" he asked as he handed back her cup.

It rattled in its saucer. "No," she said, "I'm not planning to marry again. Joshua, what's this inquisition all about? I just told you I could never fall in love a second time."

"Love and marriage don't necessarily go together," he said. "Except in the song."

"Well, speaking personally, I wouldn't consider marrying anybody I didn't love. Marriage is tough enough when you genuinely care about each other. It must be impossible if there's no love to help smooth over the rough patches."

"I'm not sure I agree with you. For hundreds of years people all over the world got married without a single thought of love in their heads. They married for companionship or for security or to have children. Or because their parents told them to. They scarcely saw each other before the wedding ceremony, and they certainly weren't in love in our sense of the word. And yet there's no evidence to show that their marriages were any less happy than the ones we have today."

"That's because expectations were different," Cathryn said shortly. "In case you haven't heard about it, there's a sexual revolution taking place, and marriage nowadays is supposed to be a loving commitment between two mature, responsible adults. It's not supposed to be a contract for financial security or a way for women to opt out of the job market or a legal way to make babies." She stood up, anxious to put an end to a conversation that was making her distinctly uncomfortable. "It's been a long day, Joshua. I think I'm going—"

"You should get off your soap box for a minute," he cut in ruthlessly, "and take a hard, clear look around. Maybe you'll never fall madly in love again, but are you quite sure you want to kiss good-bye to all the other good things marriage can bring? Don't you want children of your own? Wouldn't you like to have a companion to share your life with as you get older?"

"Yes, damn you! Yes, I want children. Yes, I want somebody to grow old with. But I can't have them, and I'll learn to live without them."

"It seems an unnecessary sacrifice."

"Surely that ought to be my own decision? Why are we having this discussion, Joshua? You're thirty-four years old and a bachelor. If you're so all-fired enthusiastic about the institution, why haven't you married?"

"Maybe I never met the right woman."

"What's the problem?" she taunted. "Are you waiting to find true love?"

There was an infinitesimal pause. "No," he said. "Not that."

"Then come and lecture me when you're married," she said. "Tell me how it works out, and maybe you'll inspire me to change my mind."

He ignored her sarcastic outburst. "There's another thing," he said quietly. "What about sex? If you don't marry, are you prepared to spend the rest of your life in a series of short, meaningless sexual relationships?"

"It's possible to live without sex," she said icily. "Celibacy is a way of life for thousands of people."

"But not for you," he said. "You're a passionate woman, Cathryn, and sooner or later your physical needs are going to get to you."

"You sound like a doctor prescribing vitamin pills. I wonder if it's my needs we're actually talking about or yours." She didn't try to hide the bitterness in her voice. "If you think this is a novel way to talk a grieving widow into bed, let me assure you that you're wrong. Every man who takes me on a date nobly volunteers to save me from the health hazards of sexual abstinence. Well, thanks, but I'm doing just fine."

"If I wanted you in my bed, I wouldn't have to talk you there."

She could feel sparks flash in her eyes. "Precisely what does that mean?"

He shrugged. "Nothing very sinister. Merely that if I wanted you in my bed, I'd have taken you in my arms after dinner, not started an intellectual discussion about the various possible foundations for a good marriage."

She had almost forgotten how burningly alive she felt when she was angry. She hadn't felt so furious with anybody in ages.

"You're not only a fool," she said, her voice tight with anger, "you're also an arrogant fool. What makes you think you've only got to take me in your arms and I'll tamely follow you upstairs to your bed?"

"Several things," he said coolly. "But chiefly this."

She had no chance to move away as he grasped her shoulders, pulling her roughly toward him. Her stomach gave a curious little leap of excitement, and then his mouth came down on hers in a hard, ruthless kiss, his arms closing around her back to press her tightly against his body.

Immediately, she felt a quick, sharp jolt of pleasure, then panic at the way her body so readily betrayed her mind every time he took her into his arms. She murmured a desperate rejection against his lips, and his touch immediately softened into a seductive, bewildering tenderness as his tongue stroked provocatively against her lips. Her eyelids drifted closed, and she felt the heat of his body penetrate her thin woolen sweater and transfer itself, throbbing and pulsing, into her veins. His hands tightened around her hips, dragging her closer to his thighs so that she could feel precisely how much she had aroused him.

Her mind spun off into a blissful darkness, leaving behind nothing but the awareness of acute physical desire. She went limp in his arms, and for an aching, pleasure-filled moment, she felt the hard, uncontrolled thrust of his hips against her thighs. His kiss deepened aggressively against her mouth, and she opened her lips, responding fiercely to the hunger she sensed in his touch. His hands stroked over her breasts, then with a sudden shuddering breath, he dragged himself completely away from her body, holding her at arms' length.

He moved quickly to the far side of the coffee table, turning his back on her as he struggled visibly for self-control. When he swung around again, the dark flush along his cheekbones had died away, leaving him pale beneath his tan.

"I'm sorry," he said brusquely, his voice flat with the effort of speaking evenly. "I shouldn't have done that. I've always despised men who exploit a sexual attraction to win points in an argument."

"Is that what you were doing?" she asked harshly. "Using your sexual expertise to make points?"

He ran a hand distractedly through his hair. "Maybe. Something like that, at any rate. I'm sorry, Cathryn."

His apology did nothing to make her less angry with him or less furious with herself. She knew only too well how passionately her body had responded to his touch. It seemed a sordid betrayal of her love for Robert to acknowledge that Joshua Hunt had the power to make her tremble with sexual need. The fact that she had the same effect on him—and that he was as reluctant as she was to acknowledge it—somehow made the situation even worse. Why did she have this persistent feeling that he didn't want to find her sexually attractive? Why did he seem as reluctant as she was to admit the strength of their mutual attraction?

She raised her chin defiantly, but she knew her attempt at laughter was a brittle failure. "Well, I suppose I ought to be grateful for your honesty. At least you don't pretend that what we were doing just now was making love."

There was another tense silence. "No," he said finally. "I know it wasn't."

His terse response tore at her painfully, but she was too distraught to analyze why. She wrapped her arms around her waist, then dropped them to her side, annoyed by the instinctive defensiveness of her gesture.

"I don't think there's anything more to say, Joshua."

"Yes, there is." She was startled by the swift urgency of his rebuttal. "Cathryn, please don't let the evening end this way. It's such a beautiful night, why don't we take a walk? There's a full moon, and the beach must look spectacular."

"I don't think I'm in the mood for a moonlight stroll."

"Why not?" He reached out to touch her, then quickly shoved his hands into his pockets. "Cathy, I can't remember when I last enjoyed a woman's company as much as I've enjoyed yours. I already know that you're a very special person, and I think we were on the way to becoming good friends until I blew it just now. I'd like us to have the chance to start over. Please come down to the beach with me."

She glanced across the room to one of the big windows, her resistance weakening. "Well, it does look like a beautiful night."

He smiled. "It is, I promise."

She followed him out of the house, and they walked across the cool grass, not touching each other as they took the narrow gravel path down to the beach. The sky was crystal clear and the full moon imparted an ethereal silver brilliance to the sea and sand. It was so quiet, they seemed to be alone in the universe. The only sounds were the crunch of their feet in the powdery sand and the swoosh of tiny waves breaking against the shore.

Cathryn took off her sandals and stood at the edge of the water, relishing the cool sensation of the waves swirling around her ankles. Joshua removed his sneakers and came to stand close beside her. They gazed in companionable silence at the vast, rippling black Atlantic Ocean. A hundred yards away from shore, waves broke repeatedly over some invisible barrier, sending a spray of white foam high into the air. The last residue of anger faded away as Cathryn watched the spume soar into the sky, gleaming briefly in the moonlight.

She bent down and trailed her fingers in the water. "I ought to wrap up some of this peacefulness and take it back to Manhattan with me," she said softly. "I'm glad you asked me to come out here with you, Joshua."

"I'm glad you agreed to come." He dropped his arm casually around her shoulders, and they splashed slowly through the shallow water, heading along the beach toward the distant lights of a small resort village a mile up the coast. A wave caught her high on the legs, drenching her slacks with cold water, but she didn't realize she had shivered until Joshua's arm tightened around her.

"You okay?" he asked. In the pale glow of moonlight, his eyes seemed dark with tenderness.

"I'm fine," she said, knowing even as she spoke that she was lying. She wasn't fine at all. She was burning up with frustration because she wanted Joshua to make love to her, and she knew he wasn't going to.

The realization was so startling that she must have shivered again, because he gave her another friendly squeeze. "I think we'd better go inside, or you'll be coming down with pneumonia."

"I'm fine," she repeated, but she didn't protest further when he walked back toward the house. The sooner she put the sea and the moonlight behind her, the sooner she would get her feelings for Joshua back into proper perspective.

They stopped only once—to wash the sand off their feet with the garden hose—before going into the kitchen.

"We're dripping water all over the floor," Cathryn said when they were inside.

"Don't worry about it. My stepmother designed the floor to survive wet, sandy feet."

There was an awkward lull in the conversation, and Cathryn could think of nothing to say to fill the silence. Her mind seemed full of pictures of the bedroom and its big, inviting bed.

"Er ... would you like a drink?" Joshua asked.

"No, thanks." She smiled brightly. "Well, I guess it's time to say good night." At the sound of false cheerfulness in her voice, she cringed inwardly. What on earth must he think of her? In addition to weeping all over him this afternoon, she was now beginning to sound like an idiot, even when she tried to make the simplest sort of small talk.

Joshua didn't seem to notice her gaucheness. "Mmm. It is late. Sleep well, Cathy." His eyes were hooded, and the fluorescent light in the kitchen, bright as it was, revealed nothing of what he was thinking.

"Sure. You too." She had turned to leave when he suddenly held out his arm, preventing her from moving forward.

"Josh?" She whispered his name, and he cupped her face in his hands, stroking a stray lock of hair out of her eyes. She saw the unmistakable flash of desire burn hotly in the depths of his gaze, but he closed his eyes for a moment or two, and when he opened them again they contained nothing more than the glow of casual friendliness. He dropped a quick kiss on her parted lips. It was as cool and controlled as his expression.

"See you tomorrow," he said. "I'm looking forward to another great day."

"You aren't ..." She swallowed painfully. "Aren't you coming upstairs?"

"No, I'll wait awhile. But you go ahead."

"Well good night, then." She was afraid that if she stayed any longer in the kitchen, she might say something she regretted, so she left in a hurry, closing the door quietly behind her. For a while, she stood in the empty hallway staring at the closed door, but there was no sound from within the kitchen. After a few seconds, not knowing herself quite what she'd been waiting for, she gave an impatient shrug and went slowly upstairs to bed.

Chapter Six

THEY WERE WALKING along the beach the next morning, looking for shells, when Cathryn heard the sounds of a car driving fast up the road toward the cottage. She shaded her eyes against the sun and saw a sleek gray Porsche come to a halt next to Joshua's red Corvette. The two cars looked good together, she thought, with their racy style and contrasting colors.

She turned to make some joking comment to Joshua, but the teasing words died unspoken on her lips. He was staring at the Porsche as if it had hypnotized him. For once he neglected to hide his true feelings behind a mask of bland charm, and the inner torment she had glimpsed so many times was plainly revealed. His mouth was drawn into a grim line, and his eyes betrayed despair.

Cathryn made some small, involuntary sound, and he

immediately bent over, ostensibly to pick up a shell. When he stood up again, his familiar mask was in place, but for the first time Cathryn wasn't deceived. She saw the tension that lingered in the taut lines of his body and recognized the effort that went into producing his apparently casual smile.

"That's my stepmother's car," he said, and if Cathryn hadn't pretended so often herself, she would never have detected the note of false brightness in his voice. "Maybe we should go back to the house and say hello."

"Is something wrong, Joshua?" she asked quietly.

"Wrong? What could be wrong?" His smile deepened to a teasing grin. "In fact, I'd say everything's terrific. My stepmother has to be the world's best cook. I suggest we threaten her with a fate worse than death unless she promises to stay and make lunch for us."

She didn't know whether to be glad or sorry that he wouldn't confide in her. "I certainly agree with that plan," she said as they walked back up the beach. "Should we hold out for something really fancy?"

"Everything Danielle prepares is really fancy," he said. "She was a domestic science major in college, specializing in *haute cuisine*."

Again she noted the peculiar flatness of his tone, and her curiosity increased. Something was very wrong about Joshua's relationship with his stepmother. Perhaps he disapproved of his father marrying such a young woman. "How long ago did your father remarry?" she asked.

"Less than a year." He paused for a moment, then added, "I didn't meet her until a couple of days before the wedding and I guess we haven't had much chance to get acquainted since. I travel so much on company business."

She had no chance to ask him anything further, even if she could have thought of a tactful question. Danielle was waiting at the kitchen door, and as soon as she saw

Joshua, she waved enthusiastically, hurrying across the stretch of rough grass to meet them. Her steps appeared to falter for a split second when she realized that he wasn't alone, but her hesitation was so fleeting that Cathryn almost immediately began to wonder if she had imagined it.

"Hello, Joshua. How are you?" Danielle said.

"Hello, Danielle." Joshua's response sounded cool, but Cathryn heard the underlying note of strain, and she could almost taste the tension radiating from his body. She was so busy speculating on what the problem between them could be that she didn't watch Joshua, and she jumped visibly when she felt his arm curve affectionately around her shoulders. She stiffened, rejecting the false impression of intimacy, but his grip tightened and prevented her from moving away.

"I'm sure you remember Cathryn Bracken?" he said to Danielle, not quite meeting her eyes. "She's a . . . special friend of mine. You met each other at dinner a couple of weeks ago."

"Yes, of course I remember her." Danielle's huge blue eyes seemed momentarily sad as she turned toward Cathryn, but her welcoming smile never wavered. Joshua's stepmother always looked pretty, Cathryn thought, but when she smiled with such obvious warmth, she became truly beautiful.

"I'm sorry for intruding on your weekend," Danielle murmured. "I didn't know Joshua would be . . . I mean, I didn't know anybody would be at the cottage. My husband had to go away on business, and I drove out here on impulse. I had no idea Joshua would be . . . entertaining."

Apart from the hesitation before the final word, there was no hint of malice in Danielle's voice, nothing except an apparently simple explanation of her presence, yet Cathryn was absolutely certain the woman was lying.

Danielle had known Joshua would be at the cottage, and that was why she had come.

The grip of Joshua's fingers against Cathryn's upper arm tightened painfully, but she was sure he didn't realize how much pressure he was exerting. "I thought you and Dad were planning to spend a quiet weekend at home together," he said to Danielle.

"Yes, we were." She turned to lead the way back into the kitchen, and Cathryn could no longer see her expression. "There was some crisis at one of the radio stations in Detroit. Your father decided to handle the problem personally."

"I see." Joshua's voice was forbidding. "He knew where I was. Why didn't he call me? I thought we'd agreed that he would leave the business traveling to me. This is his third trip in a month."

"Don't be angry with him, Josh. He still likes to feel actively involved in the business."

"Meanwhile leaving you alone at home night after night."

"It doesn't matter, Josh. Please don't worry about it."

Cathryn bit back an exclamation of pain as Joshua's fingers dug into her arm with bruising force. He blinked, as if realizing suddenly what he was doing, then released her arm.

"I'm sorry," he said in a low voice, but she suspected that he still hadn't registered how much force he'd exerted. She knew that in a few hours her arm would show a row of purple bruises.

They trooped into the kitchen, and Cathryn looked around somewhat guiltily. The pages of the Sunday *New York Times* were scattered all over the table, and their breakfast dishes were heaped untidily in the sink.

"I'm sorry," she told Danielle. "It was such a lovely morning that Joshua and I went out as soon as we'd eaten breakfast. I hadn't realized we left the kitchen looking such a mess."

"It's no problem at all. I'll clean it up while I make lunch. That is, unless you have something special planned."

"Oh no, nothing at all. Anyway, I wouldn't dare to compete with you! Joshua's already told me what a super cook you are."

Danielle blushed. "Oh, I'm not that good. Besides, it's what I was trained for. I was the house mother in an orphanage before I married, you know. That teaches you everything you could ever want to know about making second-rate ingredients into appetizing meals."

As she was speaking, she opened the small freezer and glanced into a couple of the cupboards. "How about gazpacho and a lobster salad? Honestly, Joshua, you always bring enough food to feed an army! I have to find some way to use all these vegetables."

Cathryn smiled. "I'm truly impressed, Danielle. And to think I was going to make grilled cheese sandwiches. Joshua was complaining that he never meets a woman nowadays who knows how to cook. He obviously wasn't including you on his list!"

"It's a new twist on the wicked stepmother story, isn't it?" Joshua interjected with a harsh laugh. "A man who can't find a date to live up to his stepmother's high standards."

His words caused Danielle's blush to darken painfully. She didn't seem to have taken Joshua's words as a compliment, and Cathryn decided that her earlier suspicion must be correct. For some reason Joshua didn't like his stepmother, although the evidence suggested that she had all the qualities to make a wonderful wife.

"I think I've just been severely put down," Cathryn said, attempting to lighten the mood. "Although I guess this isn't the first time a man has rejected his girl friend in favor of his mother's cooking!"

"I guess not." Danielle's reply was scarcely louder than a whisper. Cathryn saw Joshua glance swiftly at his stepmother. Their eyes met, then they immediately looked away.

"You took me too literally," he said smoothly. "No man in his right mind compares his girl friends with his mother—and certainly not with his stepmother."

He came and stood behind Cathryn, resting his hands lightly on her shoulders. "If you don't need our help, Danielle, I'd like to take Cathryn into the village before lunch. It's very picturesque, and she hasn't seen it." He allowed his fingers to trail down Cathryn's body in a suggestive caress. "We've been too busy to leave the house," he added, and the throaty undertones in his voice suggested plainly that they had scarcely left each other's arms until Danielle's unexpected arrival.

His stepmother's cheeks had been red before, but they were now almost white. "No, of course I don't need either of you." She drew in a deep breath. "Go ahead and take Cathryn to the village." She turned away to pour steaming hot water onto the dirty dishes in the sink. "Lunch will be ready in an hour, but I can keep it fresh so there's no need to hurry back."

As soon as they were in the car, backing out of the narrow driveway, Joshua turned to Cathryn. "I'm sorry about that," he said. His hands were clenched tightly on the steering wheel, a clear indication of his tension. "I'm afraid you got caught in the cross fire between my stepmother and me."

"Why don't you like her, Joshua? She seems a very friendly, warm person."

He turned to look at her, and for a moment she read blank astonishment in his gaze. There was a tiny pause before he said, "I didn't think our hostility was so apparent."

"Well, I guess anybody who was blind, deaf, dumb, and mentally incompetent wouldn't notice anything out of the way," Cathryn said dryly.

Joshua's answering smile was rueful. "That bad, huh?" The road forked, and he took the left-hand turn, driving back toward the ocean. "I want to get an apartment of my own," he said abruptly, "but it's proving ridiculously difficult to leave home. My father and I have always been good friends, but unfortunately we've had some pretty fierce disagreements recently about the way we should run the business. It's a bad time for me to announce that I'm moving out."

"I can understand that," Cathryn said sympathetically. "You wouldn't want your father to think you're rejecting him. And you certainly don't want him to suspect the truth about your feelings toward his wife. It might be pretty disastrous if he realized that you don't like her."

A long moment of silence filled the car. "Yes," he said finally. "It would probably be the final straw if my father found out how I feel about Danielle."

She studied the hard angles of his profile, then decided suddenly to take the plunge and ask him the question that hovered on the tip of her tongue. "Why did you pretend to your stepmother that we were lovers?" she asked bluntly.

Dark color ran along his cheeks beneath his tan. "I guess I owe you another apology," he said. "I seem to be spending a lot of time this weekend telling you that I'm sorry."

"Your apology's accepted, but you haven't answered my question, Joshua."

"Oh, hell, I suppose the truth of it is that I had some hare-brained scheme lurking in the back of my mind. I thought that if Danielle...if my father believed I was seriously involved with you, it might make it easier to move out of the house without causing hurt feelings all around."

"I see."

"Do you? I'm telling you the truth because I think

you can understand my problem. I hope you understand how hard it sometimes is to deal with people you love when you don't want to hurt them."

She breathed sharply. "Yes, I do understand about that."

"I still had no right to involve you in my problems. Not without asking your permission first." He stared at the road ahead, only the tightly drawn line of his mouth betraying the extent of his tension.

"Cathryn..." He broke off precipitously. "Oh, hell, forget I said anything."

"Why don't you come out with it, Joshua? We both know what you want to ask."

"It's a good thing I'm not trying to play poker with you," he said wryly. "I have the uncomfortable sensation that you can read my mind."

"Afraid I'll discover your guilty secrets, Josh?" she asked lightly.

"I don't have any worth discovering." They had driven into the village parking lot, and he pulled the car to a halt, turning to face her. "Cathryn, would you mind very much if we continued to let Danielle think that you and I are lovers?"

A sudden vivid image of herself in bed with Joshua flashed into her mind, and she felt her stomach muscles cramp with a hard twist of emotion. She stared at her hands, clenched into a tight ball in her lap. "I guess it's no big deal to help out for an hour or so."

He covered her hands briefly with his own. "Thanks, Cathy."

They spent a pleasant half-hour wandering around the winding streets of Hampton Creek. The village was a small but attractive tourist center that had once been a flourishing fishing community. The houses were all built with a rustic New England charm, and the stores had been tastefully designed to blend in with the prevailing nineteenth-century atmosphere. Cathryn found an exquisite hand-knitted baby jacket in a craft shop and bought it to send to Beth.

"Planning ahead?" Joshua asked teasingly as the saleswoman wrapped up the soft white garment.

Cathryn gave him a mischievous smile. "I wonder what you'd do if I said yes. Actually, it's for my sister. She's expecting her first baby around Thanksgiving, and I'm looking forward to becoming a doting aunt."

When they arrived back at the cottage, Danielle had cleaned the entire kitchen and was sitting in the living room sipping a drink from a tall, frosted glass. "It's Planter's Punch and guaranteed to be totally lethal," she said, holding up the glass. "Would you like one?"

"I'll fix it," Joshua said. "Don't get up, Danielle." He turned to Cathryn. "How about you, darling? Are you in the mood for a drink that's guaranteed to knock you out by the second serving?"

Her heart lurched erratically as she saw the dazzling gleam of his smile. It wasn't fair. They ought to require a license for Joshua Hunt's smiles. "Sounds interesting," she said. "You know I always like drinks where you can't taste the alcohol."

"Mmm...I remember." Joshua came and took her into his arms, then bent to drop a tiny kiss at the nape of her neck. "But I also remember what happens afterward, and we've got to get back to Manhattan tonight. So unfortunately, I guess you'd better limit yourself to one small glass."

Cathryn gulped, but before she could say anything, Danielle had jumped to her feet and offered to serve lunch. Cathryn was grateful for the interruption. It was on thing to agree to pretend that she was Joshua's lover. It was quite another to cope with the extraordinary effects his casual lovemaking had on her body.

Danielle had lunch on the table in a matter of moments. The food was absolutely delicious, and Cathryn was fervent in her praise. Nevertheless, she didn't enjoy the meal. She was painfully conscious of undercurrents swirling around her that she didn't fully understand, although she knew that they made her acutely uncomfortable. To make matters even more difficult, Danielle seemed to have no ability to talk about any subject outside her special area of expertise. She willingly gave Cathryn her recipe for gazpacho and talked at length about the problems of finding just the right lamp to match her living room decor, but she had nothing whatsoever to say about the world outside her home. Cathryn struggled to find common ground for conversation but it was heavy going, and she couldn't help contrasting the dull talk around this table with the easy, free-flowing conversations she and Joshua had enjoyed in the past.

She was more than a little surprised that Joshua made no effort to introduce more interesting topics, but he seemed to hold himself deliberately aloof from the conversation. By the end of the meal it was obvious that Danielle, despite a brave pretense to the contrary, was extremely miserable, and Cathryn suspected that for all his superficial indifference, Joshua himself was very much on edge.

She wondered again why he disliked his stepmother so much. It was true that Danielle seemed a bit wishy-washy and not precisely his type, but that didn't explain his antipathy. After all, it was Mr. Hunt, not Joshua, who had to listen constantly to Danielle's inane conversation and childishly breathless giggles. Cathryn mentally shrugged off her curiosity. The personal relationships of the Hunt family were really none of her business.

She insisted on clearing away all the luncheon dishes by herself, politely refusing Danielle's offer of help, saying the washing up was the least she could do as her contribution to a fabulous meal. In fact, her offer was not entirely unselfish. She was glad to escape to the peaceful solitude of the kitchen. Washing a few dishes seemed a small price to pay for avoiding any more of Joshua's demonstrations of pseudo-affection. It was embarrassing to feel her body quiver with awareness even when his caresses had no real meaning beyond a desire to create a false impression for his stepmother.

She took as long as she could over the dishes. When she returned to the living room, she found Joshua and Danielle sitting at the opposite ends of the room. The atmosphere positively crackled with unresolved tension, and she was sure she had interrupted an angry exchange of words. Danielle seemed to be close to tears, and she refused Cathryn's offer of coffee, saying that she needed to get back to Connecticut in case her husband returned early from his business trip. She stood up and walked to the door, looking flustered and uncertain as she said good-bye to Joshua.

"Nathan is going to his college reunion next weekend," she said, "but I think I'll be coming back here. Will you . . . er . . ." Her voice died away unhappily. "Well, don't leave anything perishable in the fridge, will you, Joshua?"

"No."

"Will you be . . . do you plan to spend next weekend here?"

"No, Cathy and I have other plans for next weekend. So you'll have the cottage all to yourself."

"Yes . . . er . . . of course. You and Cathy have other plans." Danielle must have realized that she sounded almost incoherent because she cleared her throat and began to speak less hesitantly. "Are you going to be home this week, Joshua, or do you have a business trip lined up?"

"I don't know." He swung away and went to look out

of the window. "I'll have my secretary call you first thing on Monday morning when my schedule is organized."

Danielle flinched at his curtness. She pushed uneasily at one of her golden curls, apparently uncertain of what to do or say next. Eventually she turned toward Cathryn, her smile not quite dispelling the hurt in her soft blue eyes. "Well, good-bye, Cathryn. It's been very nice meeting you. I hope we . . . I expect I'll be seeing you again soon."

"I hope so." She looked so lost that Cathryn felt the urge to comfort her. "If you ever get into Manhattan for the weekend, Danielle, give me a call. Perhaps we could have lunch together."

"I'd like that."

"But at a restaurant, mind! After the meal you prepared today, there's no way I'm allowing you to sample my terrible cooking!"

"Thanks for the compliment." Danielle smiled faintly as she picked up her slim purse and walked to the door. "Don't bother to come out, either of you. It's too hot to stand around saying good-bye."

When the sound of the Porsche's engine had faded into the distance, Cathryn turned to look at Joshua. "Your stepmother seems a little unhappy," she said quietly.

Joshua poured himself a large measure of whisky, added a couple of ice cubes, and drank it down fast. "My father is twenty-five years older than she is," he said tersely. He began to pour himself another drink, then changed his mind. "He traveled constantly for the first five months of their marriage. I guess things between them got off to a rocky start."

Cathryn trailed her fingers along the back of the sofa. "She's very pretty."

"Is she?" Joshua left the bar and came to stand directly in front of her. "Why are we talking about my stepmother? It's bad enough that she interrupted our weekend."

He cupped Cathryn's face with his hands, then dropped a quick, hard kiss on her mouth. His fingers were cold from the ice, and his lips tasted faintly of whisky. She found herself fighting against the impulse to melt into his arms and prolong the embrace.

Joshua pressed the tip of his finger against her nose. "Personally, I've always preferred slim brunettes with huge brown eyes."

"Why?" she asked tartly. "Do you think brunettes go better with your blond hair?"

He grinned. "Ouch! I guess I deserved that. Okay, Cathryn, you can stop looking indignant because I'll say it for you—women are individuals and an intelligent man doesn't judge them by the color of their hair or any other stereotyped, superficial quality."

"You're learning," she said, unable to resist answering his smile.

"Oh, I can be really quick when I have the right teacher." He glanced at his watch. "You know, we ate lunch so late that it's almost time to leave. It'll take us close to an hour to clean up here, so it'll be nine o'clock before we're back in the city. And that's if we don't run into heavy traffic."

"You're right. We should be getting ready to leave. What would you like me to do?"

Joshua had the chores for closing the cottage reduced to a highly efficient routine. They worked easily together, their methods of organization obviously similar. A cool evening breeze was picking up by the time the cottage was safely locked up, and they walked together across the narrow strip of grass, pausing at the edge of the beach.

The breeze rippled refreshingly through Cathryn's hair, and she could smell the sharp tang of seaweed and salt as it blew in from the ocean. She gave a small sigh of relaxation that changed into a quiver of pleasure when Joshua put his arm around her shoulders and drew her close against his body.

"Thank you, Joshua, for a wonderful weekend."

He looked down at her, his expression unexpectedly tender. "It has been good, hasn't it?" he said as they walked back to the car.

The drive to Manhattan seemed almost too short as far as Cathryn was concerned. Joshua directed the conversation, just as he had on the way up to the cottage, but this time she knew his attention was fully on what they were saying to each other, and she reveled in the free-flowing exchange of ideas and opinions. It was only as they approached the outskirts of the city that their talk slowed down as Joshua concentrated on navigating through the speeding traffic.

Cathryn scarcely noticed the increasingly lengthy silences. Her mind began to wander off into a pleasant daydream in which Joshua was her constant companion. He was there when she came home from work, laughing with her as they prepared dinner together. He was with her at the movies, holding her hand as the space monster gobbled up the screaming heroine. He was sitting next to her on the sofa, watching the late-night news on television. He was coming to bed with her, taking her in his arms, running his hands over her breasts, pressing her thighs against his body...

She jerked upright in her seat, horrified at the direction her fantasy had taken. The images had been so vivid that she glanced furtively at Joshua, almost as if she suspected him of reading her thoughts. He must have felt her gaze, for he turned to smile at her briefly. The tiny, crooked smile tore at her heart and twisted her stomach into a huge, tangled knot of inchoate yearning.

He would make a wonderful father, she thought, unconsciously sliding back into her daydream. He was kind and perceptive—she knew that from the way he had persuaded her to acknowledge the truth about Robert's death. He was intelligent, obviously healthy, and just about the best-looking man she had ever met. She tried to visualize his children, but found that for some reason she couldn't. Instead, she began to imagine his child growing in her womb, and she found those images so vivid that they made her breasts ache with sudden fullness.

"What's giving those big brown eyes of yours such a wistful gleam?" Joshua asked softly. "You look like an orphaned waif who's been locked outside the neighborhood candy store."

A hot wave of color flooded into her cheeks before she managed to recover her poise. If only he knew what she had really been thinking! "There's a French bakery on this street that makes the world's best croissants," she said, truthfully enough. "I *always* look wistful when I reach this corner of the block."

He laughed. "I might have known! I have a friend who's a professional photographer. He says if he ever wants to get a picture of a sexy woman looking truly sultry, all he has to do is start describing chocolate cake and fudge-ripple ice cream. Apparently it's guaranteed to produce just the right expression of helpless yearning."

They arrived at her apartment building while he was speaking, and by happy coincidence there was space to squeeze the car right outside the entrance. Although a sign said NO PARKING, Joshua pulled in anyway.

"I'd like to offer you a cup of coffee or a cool drink," she said as Joshua unlocked the trunk to retrieve her small suitcase, "but I'll understand if you want to leave right away. It's going to take you a couple of hours yet to drive home."

"I would enjoy a cool drink," he said. "It's thirsty work driving in city traffic, and the night's still young.

There's plenty of time before I need to be back in Connecticut."

Her pulses raced with an irrational spurt of anticipation at the thought of being alone with him in her apartment. For some reason, it seemed a more intimate prospect than sharing a beach cottage with him for the weekend. He put one arm casually around her waist and slipped a folded bill into the doorman's hand, asking him to keep an eye on the car. The doorman watched their progress across the lobby with ill-concealed interest.

Joshua didn't attempt to make conversation as they rode up in the elevator, and Cathryn had plenty of time to regret the invitation she had extended. Perhaps he would misunderstand her motives; perhaps he would think she expected him to spend the night. Maybe she secretly did want him to spend the night. Her cheeks flamed so fiercely at the thought that she turned hastily to scrutinize the buttons of the control panel, hurrying out of the elevator as soon as it stopped on her floor.

She felt dithery and on edge as they entered the welcome coolness of her air-conditioned apartment. Every time Joshua glanced toward her, she wondered if her face revealed some further trace of the crazy thoughts she had been harboring during the drive. Ever since the night she'd first met him, something wild seemed to have happened to her hormones. From the time of Robert's accident until the time she met Joshua, she had scarcely had a sexual thought. It was as though all her feelings of desire had been killed with her husband. Now she seemed to spend half her waking hours—and heaven knew how many of her sleeping hours—fantasizing about Joshua as a lover.

The supreme irony of the situation was that she had absolutely no reason to suppose he was considering a serious relationship with her, and even if he were, there was no way she would consider becoming seriously involved with him. Despite the fact that she desperately wanted to know the joys of motherhood and despite the fact that Joshua would make a superb father, she wasn't free to marry him. She would never marry without love, and she didn't love Joshua—she could never love anybody the way she had loved Robert. She was Robert's wife, she reminded herself fiercely, and always would be.

She put her suitcase into her bedroom and walked around the rest of the apartment, turning on lamps. When she was fairly confident her erratic emotions were fully under control, she returned to the living room, smiling brightly.

"Well, what can I get you to drink, Joshua? I have some frozen lemonade I could make up fast. Or would you like something alcoholic?"

"A vodka and tonic would taste good, if you have it."

"Coming right up." Even to her own ears, her determined cheeriness sounded grating.

He was examining the books on her shelves when she returned from the kitchen. He took the drink from her with a murmur of thanks, then put the glass down on one of the bookshelves without tasting it. In two quick strides he covered the small strip of floor that separated them and he took her into his arms. He looked down at her with an odd, searching intensity. She heard the sudden, sharp intake of his breath just a second before he spoke.

"Cathryn, would you consider marrying me?" he asked abruptly.

Chapter Seven

FOR A MOMENT she was convinced that her heart had
stopped beating.

"Marry you?" she finally managed to say. She gulped
in a life-saving gasp of air. "But we only met a few
weeks ago! We hardly know each other!"

As soon as she had made the feeble excuse, she wondered why she hadn't given him a quick, authoritative
refusal.

"Do you really think that's important?" he said quietly. "Cathryn, we're neither of us teenagers. We've both
learned to sum people up quickly—it's a requirement of
our jobs. We've had the chance to meet dozens of po-
tential partners, and we know from personal experience
that the harmony we've shared on our dates is rare. So
rare, it's almost miraculous."

"A weekend isn't very long to make that sort of judg-
ment. Not when you consider that marriage is supposed
to last a lifetime. We might find that our miraculous

harmony didn't survive very long once we were married."

"We've talked enough to know that our outlook on life is similar. Our interests are compatible. We enjoy each other's company. We're both very involved in our jobs, and I think that's an important factor. We can each take an intelligent interest in what's going on with the other person's career. But we're lucky enough to have different fields of expertise, so we're not likely to become rivals. I've heard from friends that professional rivalry can be tough to handle in a marriage."

She was irrationally chilled by his summation of the practical advantages of their marriage. "I think you may have a wrong impression of me," she said. "It's true that I've always been interested in my work, and recently I've been pretty much dedicated to my career. But after Robert died, work was all I had left. If I ever do get married again, Joshua, I want to have a family quite soon. I'm already twenty-eight, and I'd like to have two children, maybe three, and I'm sure I would want to stay home with them for three or four years at least. I don't suppose that fits in with your plans at all. I mean, from what you said, I imagine you would like to marry a woman who's really involved with her career, not somebody who's secretly longing to have a baby."

"Are you longing to have a baby, Cathryn?" he asked softly.

She flushed, angry at the unconscious self-betrayal. "I wasn't speaking personally," she said. "I was talking in general terms about the sort of wife you probably want. It seems to me that you're looking for a dedicated career woman."

"Not at all. I just didn't want you to feel that marrying me meant abandoning all your legitimate career goals. I want to be important in my children's lives, even when they're very young, because I think children deserve two loving parents, not a harassed housebound mother and an absentee father who's obsessed with his job. But the truth is, even though I hope to be an active, involved father, I would prefer that you stay home and take care of our children while they're babies. You can accuse me of being a chauvinist if you like, but I can't quite shake the old-fashioned conviction that babies probably do better if their mother doesn't work full-time. Of course I realize that in lots of families both parents need to work for financial reasons, but that wouldn't be the case for us."

Cathryn felt her hackles rise. "I agree one parent ought to stay home," she said. "Obviously young children need to have a loving person around, somebody they can count on in a crisis. But I don't see why you assume it should be me who gives up my career just because I'm a woman. Why can't *you* stay home with the children?"

"I'm sure we could work something out—although it seems to me this whole discussion started because you claimed you wanted to quit your job when we had children." He suddenly raked his hands through his hair, laughing softly. "I must say, I'm delighted at the rapid progress we're making. Here we are, already arguing about who's going to take care of our children! Do I take it you've agreed we should get married? I assume you're going to insist on a legal ceremony first, or can we start on the fun part right away? I'm looking forward to procreating those two or three children we both want. I have a hunch we're going to make the most beautiful babies together!"

She was too panic-stricken to share his laughter. Quite apart from any other considerations, it was a bit nerve-racking to find that his teasing remarks so closely paralleled the fantasies she had indulged in during the drive home. "Joshua, this conversation is crazy!" she whispered. "Fifteen minutes ago we hadn't even arranged our next date. Now we're discussing child-care arrangements for our future family! We have to slow down and start this conversation over. Somewhere along the line it went wildly off track. I can't marry you, Joshua. Of course I can't. You...I...we're not in love."

Joshua picked up his discarded drink and poked absentmindedly at the melting ice. "Are you still sure that a marriage without love is impossible, is that the problem? Does it violate your moral code to enter into a marriage that isn't based on love?"

"I don't know," she mumbled, walking a little further away from him. Her stomach churned with indecision. At this precise moment, if she was totally honest, she had to admit that she didn't know what she really felt about anything. Every time Joshua smiled at her, she was tempted to melt into his arms and forget everything except the comforting feel of his heartbeat against her breasts and the magic touch of his fingers against her skin. But elementary common sense told her that unfulfilled sexual attraction was a precarious foundation on which to build a marriage. She took a last, desperate grasp of her wavering senses, forcing herself to utter the denial that she felt sure must be true.

"Joshua, I don't know about other people, but for myself, I could never willingly enter into a marriage that wasn't based on love. I just don't believe it would work out. Not in the long run."

He put down his glass again and walked slowly over to the window. He opened the slats of the venetian blinds, and the lights of the city flickered garishly into the room, turning the beige cushions on the sofa to a dull orange and draining the natural color from his skin. Cathryn received a fleeting impression of grimness in the lines around his mouth before he turned completely away from her, staring out in the neon-lit darkness.

"I wasn't going to tell you this," he said, "knowing how you still feel about Robert." He jammed his hands into the pockets of his jeans, seeming to take a deep breath before continuing to speak. "I...love you,

Cathryn. I think I fell in love with you the first time we met. I very badly want to marry you."

His voice was thick, almost harsh, by the time he finished speaking. He didn't sound much like the way a man in love was supposed to sound, but Cathryn wasn't upset by his evident embarrassment. She felt sure she understood the reason for his uneasiness. It couldn't be easy for Joshua to declare his love so openly. Not many men would have the courage to reveal their deepest, innermost feelings to a woman who insisted she was still in love with her first husband. Cathryn quickly amended her thought. She didn't just claim to be in love with Robert; she *was* in love with him. Her love for him remained as strong and as enduring as it had ever been.

"Joshua, I do like you," she said tentatively. "I'm attracted to you physically..."

"But you could never love me, is that what you want to say?"

"Yes." She answered him quickly, firmly, not allowing a shred of hesitation to color her response. "I could never love you, Joshua."

His shoulders slumped, and for a moment she had the extraordinary impression that he was actually relieved by her answer. Then she dismissed the thought. They were both so strung out by this discussion that she was beginning to read nuances into it that simply weren't there.

He abandoned his place by the window and came over to take her back into his arms. "Isn't my love enough for both of us, Cathryn? If I love you..." He stumbled to a halt, then tried again. "Now that I've told you how much I love you, your moral scruples are taken care of. You know now that this wouldn't be a loveless marriage. You've admitted that you like me. Surely a marriage between us could work out as long as you like me and I'm...and I'm deeply in love with you?"

"Oh, Josh, I don't know. I just don't know!"

Unable to disguise the uncertainty in her voice, she realized that they both knew her resistance to the idea of marriage was weakening. It must have been the news of her sister's pregnancy, she thought, coming just at the time she first met Joshua, that had thrown the emptiness of her own life into such stark perspective. Would it be so wrong to marry him? He would be such a marvelous companion...a good father...a wonderful lover. She snapped off her final thought. Robert was the man she loved, so how could anybody else take his place as her lover?

"Please say yes, Cathy." Joshua's voice throbbed with husky persuasiveness. "I want you for my wife. I want to come home to you each night. I want us to share our problems as well as our successes." His voice deepened. "Most of all, I want you to share my bed."

She was certain that her cheeks turned bright scarlet. She stirred uneasily in his arms. "That's another thing, Joshua," she murmured breathlessly. "How can you say that you want to marry me when we've never..." She swallowed hard. "How do you know we're compatible sexually when we've never even made love?"

Joshua's laughter sounded rich with genuine amusement. He brushed his thumb across her lips until she opened her mouth. Then he leaned toward her and kissed her with tantalizing, lingering expertise. She clung to him, her fingers wound shamelessly into his hair, her breasts thrust against his chest.

His gaze was warm as it skimmed over her passion-blurred eyes. "Fortunately, I have no doubts on that score myself," he whispered. "But I'm perfectly willing to seduce you right here and now if you want me to prove that we can create skyrockets to rival the best of couples." His smile became teasing. "I think it might be a spectacular way to end the weekend."

"I didn't mean that..."

"Are you afraid I might be a clumsy lover?" he asked

softly. "I promise I'm not, but it might be a bit awkward
to produce satisfactory references!"

"I didn't mean that either."

Joshua hooked his arm around her shoulders and gently
pulled her down onto the sofa. She didn't offer any resistance when he cradled her head protectively against
his shoulder. "You know what, Cathy? I'm beginning to
think longingly of the good old days when men used to
offer marriage as a way to bribe the woman of their choice
into bed. A guy has it tough these days. Hell, just think
what would happen to my masculine ego if I made love
to you and then you turned down my offer of marriage!
I'm not sure my sense of machismo would ever recover
from the blow."

She couldn't help smiling, although her voice was a
little husky as she admitted the truth. "We both know
you have no doubts about your skill as a lover," she said.
She stared fixedly at one of his shirt buttons as she acknowledged the rest of the truth. "We both know I practically go up in flames every time you touch me."

His expression suddenly became more serious, and he
sighed. "Yes, I do know it. And I want you, Cathy,
every bit as much as you want me. You must know that
already; it's not easy for a man to hide the fact that he's
sexually aroused. But I want everything to be perfect for
us the first time we make love, and I'm not sure this is
the right moment. In the first place, my car's parked in
a no parking zone right outside your building, and I'm
expecting your doorman to buzz us at any moment. Making love under those circumstances is hardly the way to
do justice to our feelings. In the second place, I don't
want you to agree to marry me because we turn on a
great performance together in bed. I'm applying for the
position of your husband, not your friendly neighborhood
stud."

She ached with the sudden desperate longing to have
Joshua make love to her, to allow herself to become a

woman once again, with all the needs and longings that implied. Joshua's hand stroked tenderly, caringly over her flushed cheeks, and she closed her eyes, leaning back against the soft cushions. His hand moved from her face and began to roam erotically over her breasts while his mouth trailed little kisses along her jaw.

"Please say you'll have me," he whispered seductively in her ear. "Let's make a home together, Cathryn, and put the past behind us. It will be a fresh start for both of us. We can make it work, I know we can."

Somewhere in the golden haze of her pleasure, a tiny alarm sounded. Slowly, reluctantly, she pulled herself out of his embrace. "Joshua, you aren't using marriage as a convenient excuse for leaving your father's house, are you? I mean, I remember you said things were difficult there, with the disagreements about the business, and then there are the problems with your stepmother and everything . . ."

She didn't look at him until she had finished speaking, and then she saw that his face was stripped of all trace of emotion, leaving behind a cold, blank mask. Too late, she realized just how crazy her questions must have sounded. The thirty-four-year-old president of a corporation didn't propose marriage because he couldn't think of any easier way to move out of his father's home.

"Yes, things are difficult with my father," he said finally. "As for my stepmother . . . anyway, that isn't why I asked you to marry me." He turned away from her, reaching toward the table for his drink. The ice had completely melted, but he quickly swallowed it down. When he looked at her again, some of the coldness seemed to have left his eyes, to be replaced by a definite trace of mockery.

"Marriage would seem rather a drastic remedy to a temporary problem, don't you think? Bearing in mind that an alternative way of leaving home would simply be to rent my own apartment."

"I'm sorry," she said. "I guess that was a pretty dumb suggestion to make."

"Don't worry about it." The mockery in his eyes was echoed by the faint trace of amusement in his voice. "Now that you know I'm not proposing marriage simply as an alternative to a weekend spent apartment hunting, do you accept my proposal?"

"No . . . yes . . . oh heavens, I don't know." She got up from the sofa and went to lean against the bookshelf, as if greater distance could make her decision easier. "Joshua, I'm working in North Carolina all next week. Can I give you my answer next weekend?"

"If you're sure you can't give it to me any sooner."

Before she could reply, their conversation was interrupted by the buzz of the intercom. When Cathryn responded, the doorman announced that the police were making rounds, ticketing cars and towing away any vehicle left in a no parking zone.

"You'd better go," she told Joshua, releasing the switch on the intercom.

"I guess so." He grinned ruefully. "Although it's frustrating to think that a discussion of my life's destiny is being cut short by a traffic cop."

"I'm sorry to keep you waiting for an answer, Joshua. I'm not usually this incapable of making up my mind. Are you sure you want to marry somebody as indecisive as I seem to be?"

He dropped a quick kiss on her parted lips. "Quite sure. What time will you be back from North Carolina?"

"My flight lands at La Guardia at five-thirty on Friday evening."

"I'll be waiting on your doorstep by six o'clock." He pressed another fleeting kiss against her cheek. "Take care, Cathy," he said, then walked rapidly toward the door.

He was gone almost before she had time to move from the sofa. She stared blankly at her closed door for several seconds, then picked up their empty glasses and carried them into the kitchen. The rattle of the crockery against the porcelain sink echoed loudly in the empty apartment. She sighed. It suddenly seemed a long time until Friday.

Cathryn flew to Raleigh, North Carolina, early on Monday morning. She rented a car at the airport and drove twenty miles to the headquarters of Silktex, a huge apparel company. It was one of the first assignments she had handled alone, and it was fortunate that the work was strictly routine, because she seemed to have lost the capacity to concentrate. The neat rows of computer print-outs, normally so meaningful to her, seemed to dissolve into misty ribbons in front of her eyes. Several times a day she would catch herself staring dreamily into the distance, thinking about Joshua and the life they could build together. Long before the middle of the week, the fantasies had become so tempting that she had no doubts at all about what her answer to him would be. Only some lingering remnant of pride, and the deeply-rooted reticence she had acquired since Robert's death, prevented her from picking up the phone and telling him she was willing to marry him.

Despite her pleasant daydreams about their future together, she only realized precisely how much she wanted to marry Joshua when she returned to her apartment on Friday evening. As she pressed the button to summon the elevator, she felt a flicker of fear. What if he had had second thoughts? What if he'd decided he no longer wanted to marry a woman who seemed hung up on her first husband? She was amazed at how depressed she felt at the prospect of life without Joshua. When the elevator arrived, she stepped into it, feeling a hard band of nervous tension tighten around her stomach. Maybe Joshua was thinking of a polite way to tell her he'd changed his mind. Maybe he wouldn't even show up tonight.

The elevator came to a halt and almost reluctantly she

stepped into the corridor. Cathryn glanced down the narrow hall toward her apartment, and her heart leaped when she saw Joshua was already there, camped outside her door. He was seated on a canvas stool and appeared to be deeply engrossed in a paperback novel. Propped up on one side of him was an enormous bouquet of red roses. On his other side was a magnum of champagne.

He smiled as she approached, then stood up, extending the book so that she could see what he'd been reading. The cover art depicted a lady with a very large bosom and impossibly narrow waist who was dressed in something resembling a pink satin nightgown. She was wrapped in the arms of a muscular hero with black eyes and unlikely straw-blond hair. The clothes of both hero and heroine revealed large areas of tanned, well-oiled skin, although the background showed snow-covered trees and mountains. The title, *Passion Everlasting,* was blazoned in flowing purple script across the hero's thighs and the heroine's skirt.

"Hi," Cathryn said, feeling ridiculously breathless and a little shy. She smiled as she glanced down at his book. "Brushing up on your business reading?"

"Something much more important." His hand grazed lightly across her cheek in a welcoming caress, and his grin deepened. "I was getting some last-minute expert advice. If you refuse to marry me, this book explains just how to make you change your mind."

"How's that?"

"I take you off to my lair and ravish you, of course. If the first few ravishings don't do the trick, apparently I just have to keep on trying, and you'll come round in the end. Of course, some heroines seem to take a lot of persuading, but I'm hoping you'll be easier to convince than this one. I'm counting on winning you over before the birth of our second baby."

"Josh, are you absolutely sure the advice in that book is sound?"

"My dear Cathy, accept the inevitable. Marry me or prepare to be ravished. Four million readers can't be wrong."

His smile twisted her heart. "Then I guess I may as well say yes before I'm ravished," she whispered huskily, torn between tears of happiness and a sudden bubble of joyful laughter. "Oh, Josh, I've missed you this week! Let's get married soon."

"It can't be too soon for me," he said, and all trace of teasing vanished from his voice. Tossing the book on the floor, he swept her into his arms. He held her tightly, kissing her deeply, showing all the hungry passion she had yearned for.

It was a long time before they drew apart. "I think I made a strategic error," he murmured, his breathing ragged, although his tone was deliberately light. "I should have seduced you first and explained afterward why I was doing it. I guess I've missed out on a splendid ravishing."

He bent to kiss her again, and desire swept through Cathryn's body. Her hands came up around his neck, and she clung weakly to his shoulders. She felt Joshua shudder against her, and with a sudden, exhilarating awareness of her power to arouse him, she let her hands trail seductively over his body until they rested on his thighs. Feeling his skin burning beneath her fingertips, she knew her own body was on fire with the same feverish heat. When she slid her hands around his hips and across his abdomen, his self-control finally snapped. The force of his embrace pushed her back against the corridor wall, and he thrust his leg between her thighs, pinning her there as his hands pulled open her jacket and pushed apart the delicate silk of her blouse.

His thumbs brushed over her nipples, and she felt a surge of physical longing unlike anything she had ever experienced before. She pressed tightly against him, reveling in the contrast between the cold wall at her back and the hot strength of his body wedged against her breasts. Robert had never made her feel like this, she realized. Her body had never felt this wild, intoxicating longing to meld itself with another human being in the total, consuming oblivion of sexual passion.

As soon as she realized the significance of her thoughts, she was horrified. Her body froze into a solid lump of icy rigidity, and in a convulsive movement of rejection she tore herself out of Joshua's arms, scraping her back on the textured wall in her haste to be free of him.

For several seconds they stared at each other in tense silence, then Joshua spoke quietly. "What is it, Cathy?"

"Nothing. Nothing at all." She hurriedly tucked her blouse back into the waistband of her linen skirt and nervously smoothed her hair. "It's just that we're standing out here in the hallway and things were getting a bit heated. Why don't we go into my apartment?"

"Where there's nobody to disturb us when we make love?"

"Yes, yes. That's what I meant . . . that's what I mean."

He picked up the roses and handed them to her, then bent and dropped a tiny passionless kiss on her mouth. "Everything will work out, Cathy, you'll see."

She buried her nose in the flowers, rejecting his unspoken understanding of her mood. "Thank you for the roses," she said. "They're beautiful. Did I tell you they're my favorite flower? And these even smell good. Nowadays so many hothouse roses have no perfume . . ."

Joshua touched his fingers gently to her lips, cutting off the embarrassed babble of words. "Don't worry about anything," he repeated. "Let's go inside and have some champagne."

Once inside her apartment, he opened the bottle while she found a vase big enough for the huge bouquet.

"It was chilled an hour ago," he said as he removed

two fluted glasses from a cabinet, "but I suppose I'd better stand it in some ice. Champagne tastes better if it's really cold."

"The last time I had champagne was on my honeymoon," she said. For some reason, perhaps to remind herself that she could never love Joshua, she wanted to bring some mention of her first marriage into the conversation.

"I know," he said quietly. "Don't you remember? You told me it made you sneeze."

"No, I don't remember telling you that." She thrust the last of the roses into the vase, then set the arrangement on the table in the dining alcove. Her body still trembled from Joshua's lovemaking, and she was angry with him because his skill as a lover had made her betray Robert's memory. She felt an irresistible urge to flaunt the facts of her previous marriage in front of Joshua, to torment him with the knowledge that Robert had been her first lover, that she would always love Robert.

"We didn't need champagne to help us celebrate," she said. "We only took a couple of sips. Just being with Robert was always enough to make me feel high."

"I'm glad your honeymoon was such a success," he said. "You have some wonderful memories to treasure for the rest of your life."

She was too angry to pay much attention to the careful neutrality of his voice, and as he walked calmly into the living room, she felt her rage against him increase. She watched as he placed the champagne glasses on the coffee table. Wasn't he even jealous of Robert? Didn't he *care* that she kept saying she was in love with another man?

His face showed no trace of jealousy when he offered her a glass of champagne, but to her annoyance, she saw that her own hand was shaking as she accepted the drink.

"If you find that you still don't like champagne, we'll have something else," he said. "But I thought your taste might have changed in the last eighteen months." He

smiled slightly, his eyes dark with sudden warmth. "Here's
to our golden wedding anniversary," he added, raising
his glass.

His smile worked its usual devastating magic, and
Cathryn's desire to lash out at him faded away. She took
an experimental sip of the champagne, waiting for a
sneeze that never came. She sipped again, with increasing enjoyment, then sank down onto the sofa and kicked
off her shoes.

"At this time on a Friday night I'm not up to contem-
plating a fifty-year plan," she said, smiling up at him.
"Could you modify that toast a bit, please?"

"How about—here's to our first seven years? I've
heard they're the hardest."

"That sounds modest enough. I think I can cope with
that." She sipped her champagne with surprising enthusiasm and didn't protest when he offered her more. She
had eaten a snack on the plane, so there was no danger
of her getting drunk.

Joshua sat down on the sofa and rested his arm com-
panionably around her shoulders. "When are we going
to get married?" he asked.

She nestled against the crook of his arm, her anger
entirely dissipated. It was only when he started to make
love to her that she found him so hard to cope with. She
loved Robert, of course she did, but his lovemaking had
never quite made her feel the way Joshua's did . . . "How
about in September?" she asked hurriedly. "There's no
reason to wait more than a couple of months, is there?"

"No reason at all. Do you want a big ceremony with
all your family and friends in attendance?"

"Not unless you do." She looked away from him,
taking a large gulp of champagne as she tried to drown
out the vivid images of her wedding to Robert—the local
church decked out with autumn flowers; the college friend
who had flown in to be a bridesmaid, Beth in her bronze
silk dress as matron-of-honor; her mother and grand-

mother, smiling with tear-blurred eyes as she walked down the aisle on her father's arm. Oh, Robert, she cried silently, I really did love you.

She was so anxious to cut off the bittersweet memories, it scarcely registered that she had once again placed her love for Robert firmly in the past.

"I would prefer a small, informal ceremony," she said when her voice was under control again. "Would you mind that very much?"

"I'd prefer it," he replied briefly. He turned her around to face him, tilting up her chin with his forefinger. "How about next Saturday?" he asked softly. "If you don't want an elaborate affair, there's no reason for us to wait two months. There's no reason for us to wait any time at all."

She sat bolt upright on the sofa. "Next Saturday!" she exclaimed. "But that's impossible!"

"Not at all. It's not even difficult."

She forced herself to sound sweetly reasonable. "Of course it is, Joshua. You haven't considered the practical problems. Heavens, it takes my mother a week to organize a family barbecue. It'll take her at least two months to plan a wedding!"

"I expect you're underestimating her willingness to fall in with our plans," he said. "But we can get married in my father's house. You've met Danielle. She could organize the sort of simple wedding we want on a day's notice."

"But I wasn't only talking about the ceremony, Joshua! I was thinking about all the things we have to organize for the future. What's going to happen once we're married? Where will we live? What about our jobs? If we get married on Saturday and both leave for a business trip on Monday, it could be a month before we see each other again!"

"All the more reason to get the legalities out of the way as quickly as possible." He gently smoothed out the worried frown between her eyes. "We can make this apartment our main base, and on weekends we'll hunt for a house in Connecticut. A suburb like Greenwich, for example, has great family homes, and it would be a convenient location for both of us. You can commute by train to Manhattan, and I can drive to my office. It shouldn't take me more than thirty minutes, because I'll be going in the opposite direction to most of the traffic."

He refilled her glass with champagne and handed it back to her. The giant bottle was already more than half empty, Cathryn noted.

He dropped a quick kiss on her forehead, then gave an encouraging smile. "I don't know why you're still frowning. You saw how easily we solved your so-called problems."

She remained silent, although she couldn't shake the conviction that Joshua had once again cleverly manipulated the conversation off the track she wanted it to follow. His arguments sounded so entirely logical that she felt foolish in even continuing to protest, but a niggling doubt at the back of her mind warned her that the unresolved problems in their relationship amounted to considerably more than uncertainty about where they were going to live.

"Joshua, I'm scared," she said suddenly.

"Don't be. There's no reason to be frightened, Cathy. I'm going to make this marriage work, I promise you." The kiss he gave her was harder than she expected, and his words, when she thought about them, weren't entirely reassuring. He drew away from her in silence and walked quickly toward the phone.

"What we have to do right now is tell both our families about our plans," he said. "I think they might need a full week to get used to the idea of our marriage."

"I don't know about our families, but I think _I_ need a bit longer than a week." Her attempt at laughter was distinctly shaky.

The trace of hardness lingering around his eyes dissolved into a grin. "Cathy, by the end of the week you'll be wondering why we waited so long! You know what the last few days before a wedding are like."

"Yes," she agreed.

His fingers were already poised over the phone dial, but he hung up and walked back to sit beside her. "Cathy, face facts. It's never going to be easy to accept that your marriage to Robert is over. Waiting a month isn't going to change that; it will only give you longer to worry."

She knew what he said was true, but she still didn't want to hear him say it. Sometimes she was almost frightened by his sensitivity to her moods. How had he known she was thinking about the hectic week before her first marriage?

"I suppose you're right," she said stiffly, refusing to look at him.

"I know I am."

She didn't respond, and an unidentifiable emotion flickered deep down in his eyes. "I've just had a great idea," he said. "After I've called my father, why don't we drive to Valley Forge and give your parents the news in person? I'd like to meet them before the ceremony, and this is the only chance we'll have."

Introducing Joshua to her family would invest the whole idea of their marriage with a stark reality it now lacked, and that, she realized, was probably why he had made the suggestion. On the other hand, she had no desire to spend the evening alone with him. She contemplated the possibility of an intimate dinner for two in the cozy isolation of her apartment—with the queen-sized bed waiting in the bedroom—and knew it would be much better to drive to Pennsylvania. If she was mentally unprepared to announce the news to her parents, she was even less prepared at this precise moment to deal with her passionate response to his lovemaking.

"My parents would like that," she said finally. "I'll

pack some clothes while you're calling your father. But what about you? You won't have anything to wear."

"We'll stop at the drug store and pick up a toothbrush and a razor. I guess they'll have a package of underwear and some T-shirts, too."

"You certainly don't seem troubled by life's minor problems," she said. Her words were more acerbic than she had intended. She was still struggling with an uncomfortable feeling that something about their entire conversation that evening had been slightly off-key.

The pause before he replied seemed to last a long time.

"No," he finally said, "the minor problems of life don't bother me too much."

When Cathryn told her parents she was soon to be married, her mother cried soft, silent tears of happiness, and even her father's voice was suspiciously gruff as he offered his congratulations. Despite the lateness of the hour, Beth and her husband were summoned to hear the exciting news, and they came over to join gleefully in the impromptu celebration. Ken shook Joshua's hand at least a halfdozen times, and Beth claimed the privilege of a sister and kissed him with unfeigned enthusiasm. Joshua laughingly patted her abdomen and suggested she should repeat the experiment when he could get a little closer and derive full benefit from the embrace.

In fact, Joshua fitted so smoothly into the family circle that within an hour of their arrival, Mrs. Green announced that she felt as if she had known him forever. As for Cathryn's father and brother-in-law, once they learned that Joshua was a long time Pirates fan, his place in their hearts was assured. The men were soon engrossed in a heated discussion concerning baseball's designated-hitter rule. They were all in absolute agreement about its iniquities but nevertheless seemed to have endless noisy comments to make to each other. Apparently, the only thing in the world worse than designated hitters were umpires who measured the amount of pine tar oil on a player's bat.

After they had cleared away the remains of a late supper, Cathryn's mother glanced affectionately toward the three men who were still seated at the kitchen table surrounded by a clutter of beer cans. They were all talking at once and obviously deriving great pleasure from listening to themselves speak. Mrs. Green shrugged with the resignation of a lifetime baseball widow, then laughed and invited her daughters up to her bedroom. She needed help, she said, in choosing a dress to wear for the wedding.

Cathryn and Beth obligingly followed their mother upstairs. Soon they were engrossed in an earnest appraisal of every outfit that was even remotely suitable, although they all knew before they started that there wasn't a chance in the world that Mrs. Green would wear anything currently in her wardrobe for such a momentous occasion.

"And what are you going to wear?" Beth asked Cathryn as their mother disappeared into the walk-in closet in search of a silk suit.

"Oh, I don't know. Everything's happened so fast, there hasn't been time to think about minor details like my wedding dress."

"Choose something stunning," Beth said. "With your coloring, you'd look wonderful in peach. Would you come with me tomorrow and look in some of the stores here? Or do you want to choose something in Manhattan? I guess there would be more choice in the city."

"I'd like to shop with you and Mom," Cathryn said. "I'll be too busy at work to go dress hunting next week."

Beth rolled her eyes in disbelief, but she said nothing more. Only when their mother was rummaging in the closet for yet another summer suit did she say anything else personal. "I never thought you'd fall in love again,

Cathy," she murmured quietly. "I'd almost given up hope, and I'm so glad I was wrong. Joshua is a wonderful choice, and every time you glance in his direction I can see how much you love him."

Cathryn's mouth fell open. She tried to speak, but no sensible words came out. How could Beth have jumped to such an erroneous conclusion? They usually read each other's feelings with absolute accuracy.

She mumbled something incoherent, feeling distinctly relieved when their mother, freshly clad in lilac linen, emerged from the closet. It was a good thing, she thought, that her mother had appeared when she did, otherwise she might have made some remark she would have regretted later. Unless she wanted to raise a whole host of issues better left undiscussed, she couldn't tell her family that she didn't love Joshua.

With considerable difficulty Cathryn brought her mind back to the task at hand. Mrs. Green had now modeled all of her outfits. The discarded dresses and suits were piled in an untidy heap on the bed; shoes were scattered haphazardly about the floor; a hat, worn to a cousin's wedding three years ago, hung from the bedpost. Mrs. Green surveyed the wreckage of her previously immaculate bedroom with every appearance of total happiness.

"Well, what do you think?" she asked, giving a final twirl in order to display the lilac suit to her daughters.

Beth and Cathryn told her exactly what they knew she wanted to hear. They were unanimous in agreeing that Mrs. Green needed to buy something entirely new, splendidly glamorous, and probably outrageously expensive. Returning the rejected outfits to the closet, they all agreed that they had spent a very satisfying hour. Nobody was tactless enough to mention that they had come to precisely the conclusion they had all known they would reach long before Mrs. Green had taken the first dress off its padded satin hanger.

It was after midnight when Ken and Beth left for their

own house; it was almost two in the morning when Joshua put his arm around Cathryn and said gently, "You'll fall asleep in the chair if we don't get you upstairs soon."

Her parents were immediately all fond concern. "We were so interested in all your plans, we never thought what a hard week you've both had," Mrs. Green said. "Your bedroom's all ready for you, Cathryn. And you can sleep in Beth's old room, Joshua. Luckily, I put clean sheets on both beds just last week. I must have had a premonition you'd be visiting!"

Her mother laughed at her own little joke, in the mood to be happy about anything. She gave Joshua a quick, warm hug. Her father gave him a hearty clap on the back. Both of them then turned to Cathryn and gave her several affectionate hugs as they trooped toward the stairs.

"We'll just tidy up down here," Mrs. Green said. "I hate to come downstairs to a messy kitchen in the morning."

"And I still have to take the dog for a walk," Mr. Green added.

Cathryn and Joshua went upstairs together, leaving her parents to their chores. She took him into Beth's old room, leaving the door open but not turning on any lights. Silence fell around them, isolating them in a pool of quiet intimacy.

Joshua turned on the bedside lamp, then gathered her into his arms, his lips brushing tenderly across her eyelids. "You have shadows under your eyes," he said. "They make you look even more beautiful than usual."

"That sounds a bit unlikely," she said breathlessly. Her pulse was racing, her whole body alive to his touch, to the fact of his nearness. She arched her body toward him, aching for his kiss.

He brushed his mouth fleetingly across her parted lips, but when she stirred restlessly against him, he held her firmly away. "Cathy, don't! I only have so much will power." His command was harsh, and he visibly struggled for control. "It's been a long time since I last kissed my date good night wondering when her parents were going to come and bang on the door!" he said with a rueful grin. "Cathy, it's frustrating as hell for both of us, but you know we can't sleep together here; it would be a betrayal of your parents' hospitality, a betrayal of their trust."

She recognized the truth of what he was saying. Her parents' moral code was firmly rooted in the traditions of their church and their heritage. Despite what they knew went on in the outside world, in their home people slept together when they were married; they didn't sleep together before the ceremony, even if they were engaged.

Reluctantly, Cathryn moved out of Joshua's arms. "I'm sure you'll find everything you need already in the room," she said. "The bathroom's the door on your right. You share it with me."

He came with her to the door. "This time next week we'll be married," he said. "We'll be sharing everything."

The thought made her heart pound with such a potent mixture of excitement, trepidation, and longing that she scarcely noticed the odd flatness of his statement. She turned, breathless.

"Cathy..." His breathing was suddenly as ragged as hers, but he propelled her firmly toward the door. "I'll see you tomorrow," he said. "Good night, Cathy."

Chapter Eight

THEY LEFT VALLEY FORGE late on Sunday afternoon.
The good wishes and fond good-byes of her parents echoed
in Cathryn's ears as they drove along the turnpike toward
Manhattan. Her mother obviously thought Joshua was
God's personal gift to the unmarried women of America,
and she murmured repeatedly how lucky Cathryn was to
have found him. Mrs. Green hadn't been in the least
opposed to the idea of a quick marriage. As far as she
was concerned, it presented no problems at all. In fact,
she seemed to think it was only sensible "in the circumstances." She chose not to explain precisely what these
circumstances were, and Cathryn decided not to ask. She
had a suspicion they had more to do with Joshua's status
as a supremely eligible bachelor than anything connected
with her.

In his own restrained way, her father's opinion of
Joshua seemed to be as favorable as her mother's. "You
have a good man there," he said quietly as he gave

Cathryn a good-bye hug. "He's someone you can depend on."

Strangely enough, she was only partly reassured by her parents' enthusiasm about the marriage. Her own doubts were so nebulous and hard to pin down that she almost needed the chance to defend her decision to marry Joshua. Maybe if she had been forced to convince her family she was doing the right thing, she might have convinced herself at the same time.

For once, Joshua showed no particular sensitivity to her restless mood. He drove through the heavy traffic with total concentration, always slightly above the speed limit, as if he was anxious to get back to the city. His expression was remote, and the lines around his mouth appeared tight with strain, although Cathryn couldn't think of a reason in the world why their visit to her family should cause him any lingering tension. He had breezed through all the meetings with his usual devastating charm.

The traffic inevitably thickened as they approached Manhattan, and it took a long time to reach her neighborhood. When they were three blocks away from her apartment building, Joshua turned into a parking garage.

"I hope you don't mind walking a couple of blocks," he said, not really consulting her. "I can't park outside your building, because I want to come up to your apartment, and this time I don't plan to be interrupted by a traffic cop."

Cathryn swallowed the lump in her throat. "I don't mind walking."

She understood the unspoken implication of Joshua's words and accepted it. He was telling her that he intended to make love to her. The unspoken message had been burning between them all day, simmering below the casual conversations with her family, causing her skin to prickle with tension—and a reluctant anticipation—every time they happened to meet each other's eyes.

She watched the parking attendant drive off with

Joshua's car and wondered why she hadn't claimed a sudden sprained ankle or a raging migraine—anything that would have persuaded him to park his car right outside the apartment building, in the no parking zone. She wasn't ready to make love to him, she realized, though her thoughts immediately contradicted themselves. Her body longed for fulfillment, but she didn't want to accept the responsibility of actively deciding to make love. She wanted Joshua to sweep her off her feet, not ask for her willing cooperation. She wanted him to make desperate, passionate love to her until her mind blanked out and she surrendered to him in an ecstasy of blind, unthinking passion. She didn't want to be given a choice, a chance to know exactly what she was doing.

She frowned unconsciously as she took her weekend bag from him, wishing she was better at self-deception or else that she could more easily separate her physical needs from the state of her emotions. Why couldn't she just make love to Joshua and enjoy the physical sensations he aroused? Wasn't that what the sexual revolution had been all about? It was crazy to be hung up on the idea of lasting love and wholehearted commitment, emotions she knew she could never feel again now that Robert was dead.

They walked in silence through the hot, crowded streets. It occurred to Cathryn that Joshua seemed almost as preoccupied as she was, but the impression flickered out of her mind almost as soon as it flitted in. Why would he seem preoccupied? He was a man, she thought with a flash of uncharacteristic resentment. All men took their sexual pleasures lightly.

When they finally entered her apartment, she gave a tiny sigh, not quite sure whether she felt relief or resignation.

"Well, home at last." She laughed nervously.

"Yes. The trip took longer than I'd expected."

She had known things might be awkward, but she

hadn't expected them to be quite this bad. Joshua's usual sophistication seemed to have temporarily deserted him as he prowled restively around the small apartment. The cool air, mercifully free of humidity, made her more aware than ever of her hot, sticky body and rumpled clothes. Why wasn't real life more like the movies, she thought with a flash of dry humor. When a movie heroine decided to make love, she and the hero always seemed to be conveniently close to a deserted beach, where the crashing waves of the ocean pounded the shore. At the very least, they found themselves curled up on a leopard-skin rug in front of a blazing log fire. They never had to get themselves out of a rumpled blouse or shorts that had lemonade spilled on the hem. She rubbed her fingers self-consciously across the small stain, a relic of the family's lunchtime barbecue.

"I'll fix us a drink while you take a shower," Joshua said, finally breaking the unnatural silence.

"Do I look that bedraggled?" she asked wryly, thinking that the whole scene was sinking rapidly from bad farce into black comedy.

He glanced at her briefly, almost reluctantly. "You don't look at all bedraggled. You look ... very desirable." He sounded angry, as if he wished she squinted or had two left feet, but Cathryn was too overwrought to pursue the impression. She started to move in the direction of the shower, and he walked toward the kitchen without giving her a second glance.

"I'll fix those drinks," he said as she entered the bathroom.

"All right."

She gave up trying to interpret his mood and hurried into the shower, throwing off her clothes and standing under the warm, pounding water with a feeling of intense relief. The whole situation was becoming ridiculous. She knew it was crazy in this day and age for two mature people to be on the verge of marriage without ever having

been to bed together. And yet... and yet, the truth was,
she reflected with sudden honesty, she was afraid of
committing herself. Joshua was forcing her to be an equal
partner in the decision to make love, and she didn't want
to accept that responsibility.

She stepped out of the shower and wrapped herself in
a large towel. You're a total fraud, she told her reflection
in the steamy mirror. You're always talking about equal-
ity of the sexes, but when it gets right down to it, you
still live by the old double standard. You're like the
heroine in that book Joshua was reading. You want him
to make love to you, but you want him to ravish you so
that you can deny responsibility for what happens. If
Joshua seduces you, you won't have to feel guilty about
betraying Robert and the memories of your marriage.

If she made love to Joshua, she would be betraying
Robert. The thought was out in the open and wouldn't
be pushed back into the comfortable depths of her sub-
conscious. I don't love him, Robert, she cried silently,
trying to cover up her feeling of disloyalty. I could never
love anybody the way I loved you. But I want a home
and children and a friend to share things with. That's
why I'm marrying him. And you also want Joshua for
your lover, some mental demon prompted her to admit.

Not ready to cope with that particular truth, she ignored it as best she could. She removed her terrycloth
bathrobe from a hook behind the door and slipped it on,
tying the belt loosely around her waist. She brushed her
hair with meticulous care, reluctant to emerge from the
bathroom. When she finally opened the door, she felt as
awkward as a teenager on her first heavy date. Her feet
were like huge leaden weights, and the rest of her body
hovered somewhere between nervous anticipation and
total numbness.

Joshua was standing at the living room window, looking out at the glaring city lights just as he had on the
night he asked her to marry him. As she walked across

the room, he turned slowly, and a sudden flare of neon light turned his hair into a blaze of brilliant gold and outlined the harsh, masculine strength of his features in a stark contrast of light and dark.

In that brief moment, in the single flash of light, her body lost all trace of numbness. She became instantaneously aware of every detail of his appearance. She saw the tension in the taut lines of his body, one hand clenched around a frosted glass, the other hand hooked into the waistband of his slacks in a parody of relaxation. She saw the breadth of his shoulders, the powerful length of his thighs, the solid strength of his chest. She saw all of this in less than a second, and in that same second knew that she wanted him with a desire that transcended thought or reason. His gaze flicked over her body, and wherever his glance touched, her skin tingled with sudden heat.

A tall frosted glass similar to the one he held stood on the coffee table. He picked it up and handed it to her without a word, and she took a few sips before returning it to the table. Afterward, she couldn't have said whether she had drunk orange juice or neat whisky—or anything in between—although she felt light-headed as he continued to look at her.

She realized that he hadn't switched on the lights in the living room; they were looking at each other in the eerie, flickering glow of the neon signs. Gradually he seemed to fill the entire range of her vision as he moved around the table and took her into his arms. When his hands closed around her waist, she had the impression that he caught her just in time to prevent her from falling. In some dark corner of her mind she registered the fact that his mouth was grim and unsmiling as he bent to capture her lips, but the sensuous, animal heat of his body told her precisely how much he desired her, and she surrendered to his embrace with a helpless shiver of longing.

The robe slid away from her shoulders, leaving her

quivering beneath his touch. He wound her hair around his hands, and he tipped her head back to kiss her throat and bare, sloping shoulders. His mouth trailed down until it reached the hollow between her breasts. By the time he untied the loose knot of her belt and pulled open her robe, she was gasping with pleasure. She saw the dark blaze of desire in his eyes and heard the rasp of his indrawn breath, then his arms were around her again, lifting her easily and carrying her into the bedroom.

He placed her gently on the bed, then stood up and stripped off his shirt and slacks. Cathryn felt hypnotized by his simple actions. Her limbs seemed temporarily to have lost the power of movement, and only her eyes still functioned. As her gaze roamed over the hard, firm lines of Joshua's body, she felt her own body grow correspondingly soft and yielding. When he had discarded all his clothes, he stretched out next to her on the bed, and the touch of his hands and his mouth on her skin made her melt into a strange, floating weightlessness. His lips pressed kisses against her stomach as his hand went lower, slipping between her thighs and caressing them open. The soft pliancy of her body was instantly transformed into a taut bowstring of desire that flamed with heat where his fingers stroked her.

She curled her arms tightly around his neck, instinctively rasping her nails rhythmically along his spine. He leaned across her body, crushing her breasts against the weight of his chest and kissing her passionately. She opened her mouth to him, responding for the first time without any trace of hesitation. Their kiss was explosive in its intensity.

She was scarcely aware of the crucial moment when Joshua lifted himself from her side and eased himself on top of her, filling the aching void his lovemaking had already created inside her. She sighed with pleasure, opening her eyes and meeting his gaze as he entered her body, stroking her to pleasure.

His tan was darkened by a hectic flush along his cheekbones, and his blue eyes gleamed with the brilliant sheen of desire. Her body shuddered in instinctive response to this visible evidence of his arousal, and she arched more tightly against him, her fingers clutching convulsively in his hair.

For a moment Joshua held himself slightly away from her, his arms rigid on either side of her breasts as he gazed down into her face.

"I want you, Cathy," he said hoarsely. "My God, I really want you."

Something about his harsh exclamation jarred sufficiently to penetrate the fiery mist of her desire. The magic spell their bodies had been weaving together was shattered. She felt herself grow stiff and rigid with the intensity of her rejection, and when Joshua bent to recapture her mouth, she jerked her head sharply away.

Until that moment, until Joshua had said that he wanted her, neither of them had spoken a single word since they'd first come into the apartment and he had offered to fix her a drink. There had been none of the soft, inconsequential murmuring that was normally a natural part of making love. Instead of voicing words of love, they had explored each other's bodies in passionate silence.

Cathryn was horrified at the way she had responded to the expertise of Joshua's wordless lovemaking. She was horrified that mere physical passion had produced a response in her that surpassed anything she had ever felt before. Joshua was the man she had chosen to be the father of her children, the companion of her old age. He wasn't supposed to be her real love. Her only true lover was dead.

She knew he must feel the intensity of her sudden rejection, but he made no attempt to reawaken her ardor. For a moment his eyes seethed with the cold blue fire of mingled anger and desire, then the anger vanished to be replaced by some other equally intense but more fugitive emotion. He placed his hands on either side of her face, pulling her mouth roughly around to receive his kiss. A few seconds later, after a few sharp thrusts of his body, it was all over.

Joshua rolled away from her, and Cathryn lay on her back, staring up at the ceiling. After a while, he reached down and pulled the sheet over her. She noticed that he carefully left a tiny, almost imperceptible space between their bodies.

She tried desperately to think of something to say, but no appropriate words would come. She was still staring at the ceiling when Joshua spoke.

"Thank you, Cathryn. I...enjoyed...making love to you."

She bit her lip to keep from crying. It was as if he were thanking her for cooking a pleasant dinner, she thought bitterly. He'd used much the same flat, polite tone of voice when he'd thanked her for doing such a good job on the Consolidated Vision accounts. Perhaps, as far as he was concerned, making love and doing accounts were equally valuable services.

"Don't mention it. You're welcome," she replied, not bothering to mask the irony of her words.

She felt him clench his hands almost convulsively, but he made no further comment. Instead, after the briefest pause, he switched the conversation to their schedule for the upcoming week.

"I have to make a quick trip to Los Angeles," he told her. "I'm leaving on Tuesday, but I'll be back on Thursday afternoon. If you'll see about your blood test, I'll make all the other legal arrangements for our wedding. My secretary will call you if there are any unexpected problems. Could you give me a number where you can be reached during the day?"

"I'll be at the main office in Manhattan," she said politely. "It's my first in-town assignment in three months."

"Well, that's very convenient. I'll make sure Danielle has your phone number, too, in case she runs into any problems with her side of things."

Cathryn was overcome by a semi-hysterical desire to laugh. She had very little experience of how people were supposed to behave the first time they had sex together, but she couldn't help thinking that, even in the most modern arrangements, they weren't supposed to lie on opposite sides of the bed talking about work schedules and phone numbers. She turned her head, just in time to conceal two small tears that slid down her cheeks.

Joshua got out of bed. "Well, it's getting late, so I guess I should be making tracks for Connecticut. I have a breakfast meeting tomorrow morning with an aspiring producer. It's hard enough to cope with a self-proclaimed genius when you've had enough sleep; when you're only half-awake, it's impossible."

"I suppose it must be." Cathryn swung her legs out of the bed and retrieved her robe from the floor. She pulled it firmly around her body, securing the belt with a tight double knot as she followed Joshua to the front door. She wondered if he was as eager to leave as she was to have him go.

"Would you like anything to eat or drink?" she asked. "We never had dinner."

"No, thanks." He hesitated with one hand poised over the doorknob, then turned abruptly and cupped her face in his hands. His thumbs brushed over her cheeks, following the invisible path made earlier by her tears. Perhaps he had noticed them after all.

"I'm sorry, Cathy," he whispered. "But don't give up on us now. Things will work out. Trust me."

She closed her eyes, resisting the soft, melting feeling his words produced in her heart. After this evening's debacle, how could she possibly consider marrying him? Was she insane or merely a closet masochist?

She felt the quick brush of his lips against her eyelids, and in that moment she hated him because he still had the power to touch her feelings. Already her body had begun to forget the unsatisfactory culmination of their lovemaking, remembering instead the earth-shattering response his caresses had aroused in the beginning. She wanted to be indifferent to him, but it seemed that she couldn't be. Definitely a closet masochist, she thought wryly.

"I'll call you on Thursday when I get back from L.A.," he said. He appeared to hesitate on the brink of telling her something more, but in the end, he gave her another swift kiss on her mouth and left the apartment.

She wandered back into the living room, picking up her discarded glass and taking a sip. She grimaced as the liquid went down. Neat gin with barely enough tonic and lime juice to disguise the taste. With a sudden jerky movement of her hand, she raised the glass to her lips and swallowed the entire contents.

Unfortunately, the alcohol did nothing to dull the seething activity of her brain. She carried the empty glasses into the kitchen, staring blankly as she rinsed them. The hot water ran unheeded over her fingers as she finally managed to pinpoint what it was that troubled her most about the disastrous evening. First of all, even at the height of their passion, Joshua had never once said that he loved her. For a man who claimed to have fallen in love virtually at first sight, it seemed a strange omission.

But even that crucial omission wasn't the most important problem. Cathryn absentmindedly turned off the water, drying her hands on a paper towel as she forced herself to think back to the moment when Joshua had murmured that he wanted her. However many times she replayed the scene in her mind, she could still hear a note of absolute astonishment throbbing in his low voice. It was as if he had never expected to feel intense, overwhelming desire for her. Almost as if he had been as reluctant to consummate their relationship as she had been. She couldn't even shake the strange conviction that Joshua had actually been relieved when her passionate response to his lovemaking had stopped.

But surely she must be imagining things. He was a man who exuded an aura of sexuality and barely tamed virility. Why would he hesitate to make love to the woman he planned to marry? To the woman he claimed to love?

When sleep finally overtook her, she had found no answers to her questions. But she knew she hadn't allowed herself to ask the most important question of all— why was she still planning to marry Joshua Hunt next Saturday when she was no longer sure that he loved her? When, in fact, she was no longer sure of anything about him . . .

Joshua called on Thursday to explain that his father wanted to hold a bachelor dinner on Friday night. Would Cathryn mind very much if he agreed, although it would mean that they wouldn't see each other again until the day of their wedding?

Cathryn gave a light laugh and said that they had the rest of their lives ahead of them, so why would she care about a single evening apart? She assured him he was to enjoy the evening with his dad—then cried for an hour after she hung up the phone. Later that night she began to wonder if she'd contracted some weird new disease whose early symptoms were mental instability and a permanent case of butterflies in the stomach.

Her parents and grandparents, together with Beth and Ken and Annette Graham—an old friend from high school—all arrived from Pennsylvania on Friday afternoon. As soon as they had checked into their hotel, they appeared en masse at her apartment and carried her off for a prewedding dinner at the Plaza. When she protested at the extravagance, her father pointed out severely that there were times for economy and that this definitely wasn't one of them. They left her at eleven o'clock, with instructions to get a good night's sleep and a promise from her father that he would return at nine in the morning to pick her up for the drive to Connecticut. Her mother would ride with Beth and Ken. Annette had volunteered to drive Cathryn's grandparents.

She was awake by five A.M., her stomach lurching with the sort of sick excitement she used to feel on final exam days in school. She ate dry toast and drank a glass of orange juice, and the jittery pitching of her stomach steadied to the faint, regular churning she had learned over the past week to accept as normal. By the time she had taken a shower and washed her hair, she was, to all outward appearances, functioning like any other rational adult woman. Fortunately, no one could read her thoughts.

Her wedding dress hung in the closet, swathed in tissue paper. She put it on, taking pleasure in the soft rustle of the silk material as it fell in gentle folds around her. She turned quickly to view herself in the mirror and felt a tiny, irresistible quiver of delight as the dress swirled in a pale peach glow against her calves.

She went quickly to her dressing table, reaching for her tray of cosmetics. For the past couple of weeks she had lost the habit of wearing so much makeup, but today she felt an acute need for the protection that skillful makeup could bring. She didn't want people to know what she was thinking. A faint smile curved her lips. How could they read her thoughts when even she didn't even know herself what she was thinking?

She applied foundation and blush, eye liner and eye shadow, lip gloss and mascara, with all the expertise of eighteen months' regular practice. When she had finished, a cool, elegant stranger stared back at her. Only the unusual brilliance of her dark eyes gave any hint of her inner turmoil.

Her father arrived promptly at nine, looking unnaturally spruce in a gray pinstripe suit, dazzling white shirt, and striped tie.

Cathryn smiled. "I can see Mom's had a hand in your outfit," she said.

Mr. Green grinned in rueful acknowledgment. "I'm all new from top to toe," he admitted. "She dragged me out on Wednesday night and wouldn't let me go home for my dinner until I'd agreed to buy all this stuff. I've warned her that these darn shoes will probably squeak. She even made me buy new underwear."

"You look very elegant. Sort of an American Charles Boyer."

He turned pink with silent pleasure as he picked up her suitcase, which was already waiting by the front door. "And you look stunning," he said gruffly. "I've never seen you look more beautiful, Cathryn."

His words touched a hidden wound. "Not even on my last wedding day?" she asked.

"Not even then," he replied quietly, checking to make sure that her apartment door was locked behind them. "When you married Robert, you were still a young girl and you had all the prettiness of youth. Now you're a mature woman. You've learned how to cope with a tragedy, and you're stronger because of it. Then you were pretty; now you're beautiful."

For a second she couldn't answer him. "Thank you," she whispered when she recovered her voice. She pressed the button for the elevator, then turned to him impulsively. "Oh, Dad, if only you knew how immature I feel most of the time! I think I cope less well now than I did when I was younger."

"That's a sign of wisdom in itself," he said with a cheerful grin as they entered the elevator. "Don't you remember how you felt when you were a teenager? Older than time, and chock full of absolute certainty about everything. Right was right, and wrong was wrong, and there was absolutely no justification for hovering anywhere in the middle. It's a major stride forward to realize that people can rarely be certain about anything, particularly when their deepest emotions are involved."

She laughed. "You mean my dithery feeling that I'm doing something totally irrational is really a symptom of approaching maturity?"

"Honey, I'm an engineer, not a philosopher, but I think we get better at trusting our gut instincts as we get older. We spend fifteen years in school learning all the facts our teachers can cram into us just so we can get smart enough to realize that where human beings are concerned, facts are never much more than a tenth of the story."

"I think you're trying to give me a piece of fatherly advice about something."

"I guess I am. My gut instincts tell me Joshua is a great guy. And at the ripe old age of fifty-five, I've learned to go with my instincts."

The elevator came to a halt on the ground floor, and her father turned to her. "Be happy, Cathryn, and don't waste too much time worrying. Joshua is the right husband for you. I'm sure of it."

Chapter Nine

As FAR AS Cathryn could tell, the wedding was a great success with everybody—except herself and Danielle.

Danielle had turned the spacious living room of the Hunt house into a bower of summer flowers, and Judge Burris, an old friend of Joshua's father, performed the simple ceremony with friendly dignity. From the moment Cathryn stepped into their house, Joshua and his father both appeared to be all smiles, while her own family seemed to beam with equal happiness.

There were no sentimental tears from her mother or grandmother this time, Cathryn noted. Maybe they'd become a little wary of premature tears of happiness.

A buffet luncheon followed the brief ceremony, and everybody agreed that Danielle Hunt had simply surpassed herself with the meal. She had even baked and decorated a wedding cake, an incredible concoction of golden batter and spun-sugar frosting that looked like a

137

castle from a fairy tale and tasted as light as a soufflé.

Cathryn observed all the proceedings from behind a merciful haze that effectively separated her from the good-humored chatter of the other participants. Presumably she responded intelligently to her father's conversation during the drive, because he appeared to notice nothing particularly strange about her behavior. But by the time she arrived at the Hunt house, she felt mentally paralyzed and physically numb. She literally didn't feel Joshua's kiss when he bent to greet her, and during the wedding service itself she was scarcely aware of him as a person. Only his hand, burning against the bare skin of her arm, reminded her that he was real, that the words she was murmuring were binding her to another living human being.

She wasn't quite sure when her self-absorption began to decrease and she first noticed that Danielle Hunt was having a hard time pretending to be cheerful. Once she had noticed Joshua's stepmother, however, the woman's distress became rapidly apparent.

Probably because of all the work she had put in during the preceeding week, Danielle looked wan and tired, her usual ethereal prettiness faded to a haunting pallor. Cathryn was aware of a surge of guilt that was strong enough to strip away her previous feelings of remoteness. Danielle had arranged this entire wedding in a single week, with almost no help from Cathryn, who'd been tied up at work, and probably even less help from Joshua. No wonder she looked exhausted, almost at the end of her tether.

Cathryn determinedly put aside her own problems and walked quickly to the corner of the dining room, where Joshua's stepmother was standing by the laden buffet table. "Danielle, I don't know how to thank you," she said. "I already knew you were a superb cook, but now I understand why you graduated at the top of your college class. Everything is fantastic! The rooms look beautiful;

the wedding cake is exquisite, and the food is all delicious."

"Th-thank you." Danielle's pale cheeks seemed to turn even whiter. "I enjoyed doing it."

She seemed so hesitant and uncertain that Cathryn tried again to reassure her. "Everything would be outstanding even if you'd had months to prepare it," she said. "But in the circumstances, you've really worked miracles."

"In the circumstances?" Danielle whispered. She put her hand to her head, seeming to sway on her feet, and suddenly Joshua was there, his hand around his stepmother's waist, supporting her.

"Are you all right, Danielle?" he asked, and Cathryn noticed that on this occasion there was no trace of hostility in his voice, merely an odd tenderness.

"Yes. Yes, I'm fine, thanks."

Her answer was patently a lie, and Cathryn was sure that if Joshua removed his arm, Danielle would keel over.

At that moment, Mr. Hunt arrived. "What is it, Danny? Are you feeling sick again?"

"She has a migraine," Joshua said, his voice unnaturally curt. "Cathryn, could you go upstairs with her? It's almost time for us to leave, so you could change into your traveling clothes while you're up there."

"Yes, of course. Danielle, why don't you lean on my arm? I feel absolutely dreadful to think you've been working so hard for this reception that you've made yourself ill."

Danielle didn't protest when Cathryn guided her out of the dining room. They went upstairs, coming to a halt when she indicated a door painted an attractive shade of blue.

"This is my room," she said. "I'll be fine now." She turned away, not meeting Cathryn's eyes. "Thank you for helping me upstairs. I'm...sorry about...about everything."

"I'm the one who should apologize, for heaven's sake! To be honest, I suppose I was a bit annoyed with Joshua for rushing things, and I didn't even try to help you out with the preparations. Joshua insisted that you'd have no problems organizing the wedding, and I just agreed with him. I didn't stop to think how burdensome you might find it all."

Cathryn's reassuring speech didn't seem to have the calming effect she had intended. Danielle clutched her throat in a panic-stricken gesture that Cathryn had never before seen outside the movies.

"I'm going to lie down," Danielle gasped. "I'll see you . . . see you and Joshua when you get back from your honeymoon." She opened the door to her bedroom and literally fled inside.

Cathryn was still standing in the hallway when Joshua appeared a minute later. "Your case is in my bedroom," he said without preamble. "Do you remember where that is?"

"Yes, thank you." She trailed her fingers awkwardly along the stair railing. "Is it nearly time for us to leave?"

"Yes. In fact, you should change as quickly as you can. The traffic can be deadly getting out to the airport at this hour."

"Yes, I know." She intended to move, but her body didn't seem able to obey her command. She stood in the elegant, oak-paneled hallway staring at Joshua, thinking how peculiar it was to be married to somebody who, at this precise moment, seemed like a total stranger.

"I'm just going to check on Danielle," he said finally. "I want to make sure she's feeling all right before we leave."

"Yes, that would be kind."

He tapped on the powder blue door, and the power of movement finally returned to Cathryn's limbs. She turned and walked briskly down the corridor. By the time she reached the end of the hallway, Joshua was already inside his stepmother's room.

They flew to San Francisco after a noisy, high-spirited sendoff from her family, an affectionate embrace from Joshua's father, and a hearty handshake from Judge Burris. Danielle remained in her room, apparently prostrated by her migraine.

Cathryn was grateful for the innate tactfulness that had caused Joshua to choose San Francisco as the place for their honeymoon. There would be no hot, tropical beaches to remind her of the past, no soft Caribbean breezes and balmy, moonlit nights. Instead, they would have the glitter and excitement of a major city to fill their days and occupy their nights as they got used to the idea of being married.

Their hotel suite, consisting of a small sitting room, a bedroom, and a luxuriously large bathroom, was attractively decorated and comfortable. Several small arrangements of fresh flowers helped to give the rooms a lived-in, personal feeling. It was amazing how much could be organized in a week, Cathryn thought. It had taken nearly six months to plan her wedding to Robert. She picked a carnation out of one of the bouquets and sniffed it, swallowing a sudden lump in her throat.

The porter left as soon as he had finished stowing their suitcases on the special racks. Joshua took her into his arms and kissed the tip of her nose. The carnation was crushed between them. "Welcome to San Francisco, Mrs. Hunt," he said softly.

"Thank you for bringing me here, Mr. Hunt. I'm looking forward to the visit."

He nuzzled his cheek against hers. "Do you mind if I tell you again that you looked utterly, incredibly beautiful today?"

"I don't mind," she whispered breathlessly. "You looked quite handsome yourself, you know."

He bent his head and kissed her quickly on the mouth, drawing away before her response became too passionate. He looked down at her with a faint touch of embarrassment.

"Cathy, I have a confession to make, which I think is probably grounds for divorce, so I'm just hoping you'll be merciful. I know it's our wedding night, but I have to make a couple of business phone calls to Australia and I need to place them right now."

She waved her hand vaguely in the direction of the phone, not moving from his arms. "Be my guest. See what a perfect wife I am? Not even a murmur of complaint."

"Definitely a perfect wife." He gave her another quick kiss. "But these calls require concentration, Cathryn, and I'm afraid I find you very distracting." His smile was disarming, his gaze tender. "Could you spend fifteen minutes in the bedroom or the bathroom while I use this room for my calls? I've made dinner reservations at the Marguerite for eight o'clock, and once this... business... is completed, I swear I won't even think about the office or the cable television industry for all of next week."

"I'll hold you to that," she said, returning his smile as she walked toward the door. "For the rest of the week, any mention of business is strictly off limits. Agreed?"

"Agreed."

She closed the door between the two rooms, actually feeling a little relieved to have a few minutes alone. Plane journeys always made her feel hot and tired, and she wanted to take a quick shower. Even though this wasn't exactly the romantic match of the century, for some reason she wanted to look attractive tonight, and she was still much too self-conscious to feel comfortable changing in front of Joshua.

She opened her suitcase and removed some of her clothes. Despite all her claims of frantic overwork at the office, she had found time to buy several new dresses for her honeymoon.

She selected a white voile dress sprigged with yellow flowers, laying it out on the bed. At first glance, its styling appeared deceptively young and innocent. At second glance, its sophistication became apparent. The sheer fabric hinted alluringly at her body only half-concealed beneath the filmy folds, while the thin shoulder straps and low-cut back made it clear that she wore neither bra nor camisole.

Joshua's reaction fifteen minutes later was all she had hoped for. She was sweeping her hair into a loose knot of curls on top of her head when he entered the room. He stopped dead in his tracks, his glance meeting hers in the mirror. Several emotions that she couldn't interpret chased across his face, but there was no mistaking the hot gleam of appreciation and desire that finally darkened his eyes.

Her heart pounded against her ribcage. Her hands seemed glued to her hair. "Phone calls all finished?" she managed to ask, with an attempt at casualness.

"Yes." He cleared his throat. "I had a quick word with my father, too. And with Dani . . . my stepmother. Just to let them know we'd arrived safely. He's invited your parents to spend the night there."

"That's thoughtful of him." She put the last pin into her hair and stood up, turning to face him. She knew that the light on the dressing table shone behind her, silhouetting her figure through the thin fabric of her dress. At the harsh rasp of Joshua's indrawn breath, she felt a reckless, heady surge of excitement.

She walked halfway across the room. "Do you like my dress?" she asked, turning slowly, deliberately allowing the light to reveal the shadowy contours of her body.

He said nothing at all, and she repeated her question. "Do you like it, Joshua?"

"It's beautiful; you're beautiful. I've said that a dozen times today already, but there's nothing new for me to say." For a moment his mouth seemed to tighten. "You must know you're a very desirable woman."

She halted only inches away from him. "I'm glad you think so," she said huskily.

Briefly she thought he was going to kiss her, and her lips parted in involuntary anticipation. His eyes blazed with the unmistakable fire of passion, but he drew away from her, picking up a light wrap from the bed and draping it across her shoulders.

"I know they won't hold those dinner reservations for us, so we'd better hurry," he said. "Are you hungry?"

She laughed, covering her disappointment that he hadn't kissed her. "I'm probably supposed to say, 'Darling, not for food.' But the truth is, I'm starving. Somehow I never seemed to get around to eating any of those marvelous goodies Danielle made for the wedding reception."

"No, neither did I." There was a tiny pause. "Well, we'll make up for it tonight. I think the Marguerite has the best food in San Francisco, and since this city has some of the finest restaurants in America, that's quite a claim."

They ordered chicken breasts stuffed with lobster and poached in wine, followed by crusty chocolate soufflés split open and served with hot, melted chocolate. Over their second cups of espresso coffee, Joshua suggested they go to a nightclub that was located practically next door to the Marguerite and was known for its excellent band.

"A few hours of dancing sounds like a terrific idea," Cathryn agreed ruefully. "In fact, after that huge meal, a week of hard exercise might be more appropriate."

"The food was good, wasn't it?"

"Mmm...delicious," she murmured as they made their way outside.

The sudden shock of cool air made Cathryn realize that she had consumed considerably more wine than she had intended. Her legs felt distinctly wobbly, and she leaned instinctively against Joshua, seeking support. After an infinitesimal hesitation, he put his arm around her waist, drawing her head down to rest on his shoulder. The wobbly feeling in her knees immediately increased, and she finally acknowledged what she had subconsciously recognized hours earlier. She wanted Joshua to make love to her again. She felt almost feverish with the longing to have his naked body next to hers.

When they reached the entrance to the nightclub, she stumbled slightly as they crossed the threshold. She knew it wasn't the wine that was making her so clumsy.

Joshua's arm tightened around her waist. "Are you okay?" he asked.

"Fine." As fine as she could be when her body was aching for his touch, his possession.

The interior of the nightclub was dark except for the dance area, which vibrated under the brilliant, shifting glow of multicolored strobe lights. They ordered drinks, which neither of them touched, then Joshua led her out onto the dance floor.

He was an excellent dancer, and for a while Cathryn was able to lose herself in the pounding rhythms of the music. After a while, the live band took a break, and the strobe lights were dimmed to a soft, muted pink glow. The music, now presumably taped, slowed and quieted.

She heard Joshua make some small, inarticulate sound deep in his throat, then he gathered her into his arms and pressed her tightly against him. She let her head rest against his chest as his hands moved with exquisite, hesitant lightness over her hair. The entire surface of her skin seemed to dissolve into a formless mass of tingling nerve endings, and she felt herself begin to shake when Joshua's body hardened unmistakably against her pelvis.

"I think it's time to go," he said thickly, his hands tight against the small of her back.

"Yes." She slumped against him in unspoken surrender, unable to disguise her emotions any longer. They completed the taxi drive back to the hotel in silence, sitting as far away from each other as they could, almost as if they were afraid of what might happen if their bodies touched accidentally.

Even when they were inside the hotel suite, they stayed a little apart, carefully preserving the six inches of dark brown carpet that kept their feet separated. The air between them seemed weighted with significance—a few inches of space that yawned as wide as a mountain chasm. Cathryn had the eerie feeling that once the gap between them was closed, she would never be able to open it again.

The emptiness of the air gradually filled with un-bearable tension, swelling in the unnatural silence until Cathryn felt she could hardly breathe. She lifted her hand to her throat, and the tiny movement was enough to ignite the blaze that was waiting to consume them both. The clear blue of Joshua's eyes turned to a smoky gray, and his mouth came over hers like an explosion, driving the breath back into her body and propelling them both onto the bed.

"I want you," he murmured against her mouth. "I want you so much that it hurts. I want to possess your lips, your breasts, your kisses . . . all of you. I want to make you soft with passion, to make love to you until your body is on fire for me—only for me."

"I want you too," she whispered harshly.

The words were out, the truth acknowledged. Her fingers tightened in a convulsive grip on his shoulders and her lips parted, welcoming the thrust of his tongue. In some obscure corner of her mind she recognized the totality of her surrender, but consciously she knew only that she was giving herself to him because he had left her with no will to resist. His touch, his kiss, the hard length of his body burning against hers, aroused her to a point where she was aware of nothing save the fierce reality of her own desire.

She watched as he pulled off his jacket and tie, realizing that he was unbuttoning his shirt with almost savage impatience. He returned to the bed, and his searching fingers found the pins holding up her hair, pulling them out with shaking fingers. He buried his face in the lush, thick mass and breathed a ragged sigh. Then he reached for the concealed zipper on her dress and pulled it ruthlessly open. Slowly he pushed the dress down her body, his mouth following the path traced by his hands. When her clothes lay in a heap at the foot of the bed, his gaze traveled hungrily over her, sweeping up her long, slim legs and resting demandingly on the delicate flare of her narrow hips and the curve of her full breasts. He wasn't even touching her, but already he was making her body tremble with intense, overwhelming need.

She closed her eyes, knowing that she must shield herself from his scrutiny, although she wasn't sure what she was trying to protect. The urgency of her need for him made clear thinking impossible. She heard the rustle of Joshua's remaining clothing as it fell to the floor, then felt the bed dip as he returned to her side. She moved toward him, opening her eyes again, and he reached out to caress her face with fingers that shook visibly.

"Oh God, Cathy," he murmured. "Why do you have to be so damn beautiful?"

"For you," she whispered. "Only for you. So that you'll make love to me."

Almost before she finished speaking, his mouth came down hard on hers. Flushed, feverish with desire, she opened her mouth, submitting willingly to the insistent sensuality of his kiss. When he finally drew away, the aching rasp of his breath seemed to pound in rhythm with the dark heat that pulsed within her.

The air felt cold where he had left a tiny space between them, and she reached up to pull him close again, winding her hands in the springy thickness of his hair as she guided his mouth to her breast. She felt him shudder as he sucked gently, curling his tongue around each nipple, and her body softened in welcome.

Her need for him was a throbbing void, yearning to be filled, and she felt herself trembling on the verge of an incredible new world of pleasure. She had never felt this way before.

"Love me, Joshua," she whispered. "Please love me now. Don't wait."

The hard, demanding passion of his expression melted into tenderness. "Believe me, darling, there's no way I could wait any longer."

Darling. The husky caress of the word echoed in her mind as he put his hands beneath her hips and lifted her up to accept his body. She thought he whispered it again as he eased inside her, filling her emptiness with his urgent need. She closed her eyes, wanting to block out the world and feel nothing except the desire that wrapped them both in its shimmering folds, nothing except the heat that fused their two bodies into one perfect whole.

"Darling." She heard him murmur the endearment against her mouth as she reached her final, shattering climax, and the soft sound of the word intensified her pleasure into a cataclysmic explosion of joy.

But when passion was slaked and their bodies finally grew still, he had no more words of love to give her.

He withdrew from her in silence, although he didn't move very far away and their bodies remained curled together in the middle of the big bed. He touched her cheeks, cradling her face in his hands.

"No tears this time," he said softly. "I'm glad." He

kissed her passion-swollen lips. "Good night, Cathy. Sleep well."

She had no idea why her heart suddenly felt as if it were too big to fit her body. She drew away from the disturbing touch of his fingers, rolling onto her stomach before she spoke.

"Good night, Joshua."

She waited until she was certain he was asleep before she got up and locked herself in the bathroom, where she cried for twenty minutes without stopping. When she was finally in control of herself again, she reflected wryly that whatever strange affliction she had contracted since meeting Joshua, marriage certainly didn't seem to be the cure.

The next day set the pattern for the rest of their honeymoon. They breakfasted late in their room, then set out to view the tourist sights of the city. Joshua had visited San Francisco before, but Cathryn had never been there. The weather was kind to them, unusually sunny but not unbearably hot, and they toured enthusiastically from the Presidio—the original Spanish garrison area—to Fisherman's Wharf to Chinatown. On subsequent days they drove through the chain of redwood groves along the Redwood Highway, sampled the wine in the vineyards of the Napa Valley, and traveled south to San Jose, the oldest incorporated town in California.

The instantaneous rapport that had been theirs from the beginning never deserted them during these tours. Conversation flowed easily, and Cathryn knew that Joshua derived as much pleasure as she did from the constant exchange of ideas and opinions about every subject under the sun. There seemed to be only two subjects that were forbidden—they never discussed their feelings for each other, and they never discussed what happened each night in the darkened intimacy of their hotel bedroom.

Cathryn released him from his promise not to discuss

work, and he gradually confided a lot more about his professional problems. He explained that his father had only reluctantly resigned from the presidency of Consolidated Vision when he discovered that Danielle couldn't cope with a husband who was always traveling. He had never relinquished active financial control of the company, however, and Joshua was still struggling to get the power that would match his impressive job title.

For six months he had been fighting a wearisome battle to convince his father that the radio and television marketplace had changed drastically over the last five years and that their company needed an equally drastic change in its approach to the market.

Cathryn had no difficulty reading between the lines of Joshua's confidences, and she gradually realized that he had been driven almost to the point of exhaustion by the constant, frustrating opposition from his father. She offered him what advice she could, drawing on her knowledge of the world of finance, and felt a warm glow of pleasure when he acknowledged the usefulness of her suggestions. It was a relief for him, he admitted, simply to have somebody to talk to.

"What your father needs is a new interest," Cathryn said as they ate lunch at a bayside restaurant on the last day of their honeymoon.

She swallowed a bite of shrimp, smiling at a sudden pleasant idea. "You know, Danielle is a young woman and your father is only in his early fifties. Maybe they'll start another family. A baby to coo over would be guaranteed to take your dad's mind off his business worries."

There was such a long silence that she was afraid she had offended him. On second, wiser, thought, she could well understand that Joshua wouldn't relish the prospect of a step-sibling who would be thirty-five years younger than he was. She wished, too late, that she had stopped to think before speaking. During the last six days, she realized, she had lost the habit of censoring her own conversation.

"Danielle had a miscarriage last February," Joshua said finally. "I think I told you that I met her for the first time on the day she married my father, then they went off for a three-month trip to Europe. When they came back, my father began to travel constantly. He was trying to make up for lost time, I guess, and maybe trying to show everybody he was still actively in charge of the company, even though I'd been running things while he was in Europe. He'd been away for three weeks when Danielle started to miscarry. She had no family in Connecticut, so even though we were virtually strangers, I had to take her to the hospital and hold her hand while she lay in the emergency room losing her baby. And I was the one who had to comfort her when it was all over."

"Why didn't your father come home?"

"We knew he was in Tokyo, but he switched hotels unexpectedly so we couldn't reach him for nearly twenty-four hours, and then he couldn't book a flight out for another eighteen hours. It was more than three days before he finally arrived home, and Danielle was out of the hospital by then. She had to go through that whole rotten experience without her husband."

"She had you. She had her husband a few days later. That's better than having nobody."

Cathryn hadn't meant to let any trace of emotion sound in her voice, but she had forgotten how sensitive Joshua could be to her moods, and he looked up at her at once, a strange expression shadowing his eyes. *"You* had a miscarriage? You miscarried Robert's baby?"

"Yes." Once made, the admission opened the festering wound of her loss, and the words came tumbling out, flat and leaden with pain.

"Knowing that I was carrying Robert's child was the only thing that kept me going for the first few weeks after he died. I lost our baby just before Christmas." She heard herself laugh and caught the black tinge of bitterness in the sound. "The doctor on duty that night was one of those hearty types. He thumped me on the back and told me the miscarriage was all for the best. Nature's way of correcting one of its mistakes. He said there would be lots of other healthy babies to take the place of the one I'd lost."

She scarcely heard the violent imprecation Joshua muttered under his breath. "I hope your father punched the doctor clean on his arrogant, unfeeling nose," he said. "Better yet, I hope you punched him yourself."

"My family didn't know what had happened. When I went home, they thought I was so distraught because it was the first Christmas holiday I'd spent without Robert."

"You went through the miscarriage completely *alone?* For God's sake, Cathy, why? Why didn't you tell your parents what was going on?"

"They hadn't known I was pregnant, and it seemed the wrong moment to tell them." She looked away, blinking back tears as she stared out across the bay. Eighteen months without a tear, she thought, and since she'd met Joshua she couldn't seem to keep her eyes dry.

"You shouldn't have tried to carry that loss alone," he said.

"I don't know if you can understand—I don't know if anybody could be expected to understand—but my pregnancy was sort of a last secret I shared with Robert. When I started to miscarry..." She swallowed hard. "Some things hurt too much to share with anybody. I didn't feel strong enough to cope with my family's grief. I could barely cope with my own."

His hand reached out to cover hers, warm and strong and caring. "I love you, Cathryn," he said. "I'll always be here for you."

She felt an answer trembling in her throat, but no

sound emerged. Emotion welled up from deep inside her and turned slowly to desire as they looked at each other across the table. Wordlessly, Joshua got up, pulling her with him and tossing a couple of bills onto the table to pay for lunch.

Outside the restaurant, he raised his hand to summon a cab. One instantly swerved from the far side of the road and braked to a halt beside the curb.

"I've never seen that happen before," Cathryn said, trying to lighten the tension between them. "What's your secret?"

"I think the driver must have sensed my urgency." He tangled his hand in her hair, then drew sharply away from her. "Touching you is more than I can handle right now. Thank God we're not far from the hotel."

As soon as they were inside their suite, he took her into his arms, kissing her with a tormented, aching hunger. He pulled her down onto the bed, reaching immediately for the buttons of her thin muslin blouse. Placing her hand over his, she captured his unsteady fingers.

"I'll do that," she whispered. "You just watch."

She slipped off the bed and stood beside it, slowly pushing each small button out of its hole. When all the front fastenings were undone, she allowed the blouse to slide down her shoulders. Joshua's chest started to rise and fall in a rapid, jerky movement, and she leaned over him, letting her nipples graze his skin. "Undo my bra," she commanded huskily.

His fingers were shaking as he reached for the front closing, and a flush of color washed up to darken his cheeks when she tossed the bra to a corner of the room. He reached up to pull her back onto the bed, but she wriggled out of his grasp, stripping off the remainder of her clothes with the same deliberate provocation she had used for her blouse. She had never undressed solely with the intention of teasing a man before, and she found the hungry passion of Joshua's gaze intensely exciting.

When all her clothes were gone, scattered in a heap around her ankles, she shook her hair free of its combs, and it fell in a heavy sweep around her face.

With a low groan, Joshua sprang off the bed, pulling her into his arms. "That's all I can stand," he said. "Don't you know a man could die of that sort of torture?"

She twisted delicately against him. "But think of it, Josh. What a fabulous way to go!"

"I can think of more satisfying ways," he murmured, holding her so tightly that her breasts were flattened against him.

He kissed her with almost brutal urgency as she helped him take off his clothes, exploring his body with increasing eagerness until he lifted her and set her with unexpected gentleness onto the bed. He knelt over her, his hand caressing her until he felt the betraying shudder of her body.

He stroked the sweat-dampened hair away from her forehead. "I'm glad it's daylight," he said. "I like to look at you while we make love."

He ran his fingers lightly across her inner thigh, smiling slightly as she quivered in response. "Do you know your eyes turn a wonderful violet when I touch you here?"

She felt herself blush with mingled embarrassment and pleasure. "I have brown eyes," she said huskily. "Maybe hazel. Nobody has violet eyes."

"You haven't seen yours when I'm making love to you." He pulled her close against him, wrapping his arms protectively around her.

"I want you," he said, and the demanding urgency of his voice caused her desire to spiral out of control. Her hips arched wildly in response to his movements. She felt the gasp of his breath against her mouth, the hard thrust of his body against hers, and then pleasure convulsed her, sending her conscious thoughts spinning away into the warm, waiting darkness.

Chapter Ten

THEY LEFT SAN FRANCISCO on Sunday morning, but because of the time difference it was early evening when they arrived back at her apartment. They picked up cold meats and a variety of cheeses at a corner delicatessen, then walked to the French bakery and bought hot, crusty rolls and chocolate-filled croissants for dessert. They spread their goodies over the small table in the dining room, and Cathryn thought that she had never eaten a meal that tasted so good. After dinner, they went down to the basement laundromat and washed all the clothes from their honeymoon, then laughed as they argued about where to fit Joshua's belongings into drawers and cupboards that were already too full.

"Now I know exactly why you married me," he muttered, abandoning his useless attempt to find room inside the bedroom closet for the only business suit he had brought with him. Resignedly, he hooked the suit hanger over the molding on the bathroom door.

"Why did I marry you?"

"You needed more closet space and latched on to the first man who suggested buying a house. To think after all these years of searching for a woman who'd love me for myself, I ended up being caught by a woman who was just looking for a comfortable home in the suburbs."

"Is your ego irreparably shattered?"

"Not irreparably, I guess. I suppose there are ways you could find to make me feel better."

Her breath caught in her throat. "Does it help if I admit I didn't *only* marry you for the extra closet space? There were . . . there were a couple of other reasons."

"I hope they were the right ones." He leaned against the bathroom door, regarding her intently. The cheerful banter faded into absolute stillness. "Why did you marry me, Cathy?"

An answer was forming in her mind, an answer she didn't want to give, so she spoke quickly, before the fatal words could come out. "Because I want you," she said. "I wanted to have you around to make love to me every night."

For a moment Joshua didn't move, then in two swift strides he was beside her, his hands seizing her hair and pulling her head back to receive his kiss. "If that's what you wanted, lady, then that's what you'll get."

She saw the anger of his words duplicated in his expression, along with a desire he didn't attempt to hide. The force of his kiss seemed expressly designed to stamp her with the seal of his possession.

He didn't bother with any of the tender, seductive preliminaries she had come to expect from him. He took her with an almost desperate intensity, and she answered him with an urgency that was equally as overwhelming, feeling amazed and a little frightened by the stormy violence of her response. Their passion was spent too quickly to satisfy either of them, and they turned to each other once again, seeking solace in a more sensual, slower lovemaking. But their restraint didn't last long, and in the end they held each other with the same desperate, clinging desire.

Joshua fell asleep almost immediately, and Cathryn lay still, staring at the shadowy outline of his suit hanging on the bathroom door. Feeling him stir lightly against her, she instinctively curled her body against his, luxuriating in the smooth, muscular feel of his hips as they curved into the soft hollow formed by her stomach and thighs. Moments later, he rolled over onto his stomach, giving an unglamorous little snort that sounded a bit like the snuffling of a young baby. At that precise moment Cathryn realized how much she loved him.

She loved him completely and absolutely. Not with the warm, comfortable security of the love she had had for Robert, but with a different and more painful kind of love.

She propped herself up on one elbow, allowing her hands to drift lightly down the hard length of his body. Finally she understood that it was no betrayal of Robert's memory to admit to herself that she could love another man. It was only because she and Robert had shared the carefree happiness of two young lovers that she was now capable of experiencing the richness and depth of her feelings for Joshua. She pressed a soft, silent kiss against his shoulder, wondering how she had ever doubted that there could be room in her life for two loves. Loving Joshua didn't mean that she had to deny her feelings for Robert. He would always be a much-loved part of her past, an integral part of her being, but Joshua was the man she loved now.

Suddenly Joshua poked out his arm and dropped it unceremoniously around her waist. "Love you," he mumbled, obviously still more than three-quarters asleep.

"I love you too," she said, but she knew he didn't hear her.

Breakfast the next morning was a mad scramble as they tried to get ready to set off in two different directions without falling over each other in the limited space of the bathroom and kitchen. Joshua carried his coffee cup and a bowl back to the sink, dropping a friendly kiss on the nape of her neck when they met in the kitchen doorway.

"Now I know I love you," he said. "Only the truest of true love could get me to swallow unsweetened yogurt for breakfast without complaining."

"It's good for you." She laughed and glanced up at him, her heart aching with unexpressed love. She wanted to make the simple admission, to tell him that she loved him as much as he seemed to love her. But he was already walking away, picking up his briefcase and shrugging into his jacket. The moment hardly seemed right for a passionate avowal of her deepest feelings. He leaned over and pecked her cheek before leaving the apartment.

"I'll be here on Friday night," he said. "What time will you be back?"

"I'll be home from the airport by seven."

His hand caressed the curve of her cheek. "I'll be here before then. Don't be late." He started out the door, then suddenly he swung back, kissing her hard on the lips. "Take care of yourself and don't forget to call me every night."

He sprinted to catch the elevator that had just stopped on their floor, not looking at her again before the doors swooshed closed.

Cathryn was scheduled to spend Monday morning at the main office before catching an early afternoon flight to Michigan. When she walked into her cubicle, she found a big box wrapped in shiny silver paper waiting on her desk together with an interoffice memo indicating that she was wanted immediately in Mr. Marlowe's office.

Mr. Marlowe was the senior partner of Kingston and Arthur, a being so superior and exalted that so far she had never spoken with him directly. Their acquaintance had been limited to remote smiles on his side and respectful nods on hers. She tapped on his impressive oak door with considerable trepidation.

He told her to come in and smiled amiably as he greeted her. "Ah, Mrs. Hunt, good morning. You look very well, radiant in fact. I·gather your honeymoon agreed with you?"

"It was wonderful. The only trouble was that it ended much too soon." Surprise at seeing the dignified Mr. Marlowe in his shirtsleeves made her speak without thinking.

His smile merely widened. "Work didn't seem very appealing this morning, I gather. Well, I have a suggestion that may help your problem. I have a small gift to offer you on behalf of the company. We've flown somebody from our Chicago office to Michigan, and he'll take over your assignment at General Merchandise. Please take the next week off as an extra vacation. You can consider the free time as a wedding present from the senior partners at Kingston and Arthur."

Surprise and happiness transformed her expression. "Why, thank you, Mr. Marlowe! That's a fantastic wedding gift, the best one you could have given me, and I'm very grateful for your thoughtfulness. I know how busy we are right now."

"You've worked hard and extremely efficiently. I'm pleased to have a chance to show my appreciation in a practical way." His intercom buzzed, and his expression returned to the usual one of austere concentration. "Good morning, Mrs. Hunt. Don't take too long leaving or I may yet find you another assignment."

She escaped from his office only to find a small crowd of her colleagues waiting around her desk. To the accompaniment of several ribald remarks, she opened the silver-wrapped package and found it contained a sixty-piece set of bar glasses.

"That's so you can invite all of us to a party in your new home," Jim said. "No excuses. And we expect the best now that you've married money."

"You're not exactly subtle in your hints, are you?" she teased.

"I've decided subtlety is the wrong approach with you."

There were several more laughing comments as she thanked everybody warmly for their gift.

People drifted back to their desks until only Jim was left in her small office. "I don't have to ask if you're happy," he said. "You look positively radiant, Cathryn."

"I feel that way, too." She picked up the huge carton of glasses. "Have you any idea how I'm supposed to get this back to my apartment? I've already got a suitcase to take back with me."

"I'll come downstairs with you and organize a cab. Joshua Hunt may have worked wonders on your smile, but he seems to have robbed you of your usual sharp efficiency."

When she arrived back at her apartment, it seemed both cramped and lonely. She dumped her box of bar glasses on the table and reached for the phone, planning to call Joshua and tell him the good news about her extra vacation time. But she stopped halfway through dialing his office number. Why call him when she could go directly to his father's house and surprise him?

She acted upon the idea as soon as it came to her, changing quickly into navy blue cotton pants, a white muslin shirt, and white sneakers, pulling the pins out of her hair and tying it back loosely with a blue silk scarf. She grabbed the suitcase she had prepared for her business trip to Michigan, not bothering to repack it, and caught a cab to Grand Central Station.

There was almost an hour's wait before the next train to Waterford, and she passed the time buying the sexiest black nightgown she could find—with lace-trimmed holes cut in the unlikeliest places. Or perhaps the likeliest places, she thought, smiling softly as she transferred the nightgown from its package to her suitcase.

It was only mid-afternoon when the cab driver dropped her off at Joshua's house, and she didn't expect to find him at home. Sure enough, the doorbell was answered by the daily cleaning lady, who said that Mr. Hunt senior and junior were both at work. Mrs. Hunt was at home, however. She was out in the backyard, weeding the vegetable garden.

"Don't disturb Mrs. Hunt," Cathryn said. "I know how frustrating it is when you're in the middle of some chore and visitors arrive. I'll go up to Joshua's bedroom and unpack my suitcase. When Mrs. Hunt comes in, would you please let her know that I'm here?"

"Sure thing. And she's fixing roast leg of lamb for dinner, so it won't be a bit of trouble to add one more serving. She hasn't been feeling too well this past week, so it's better not to disturb her now she's worked up the energy to get out in the sunshine."

The cleaning woman returned to the kitchen, and Cathryn walked quietly up the elegant staircase, her sneakered feet making no sound on the thickly carpeted floors. She recognized the door to Joshua's room without difficulty. It was located at the end of the corridor, somewhat away from the rooms occupied by Danielle and his father.

She put down her suitcase and pulled off the silk scarf that confined her hair, running her hands through the long, thick strands. The air-conditioning in the train hadn't been working well, and she was looking forward to taking a shower before Joshua got home from work. She was just about to open the door when she heard a faint sound from inside the room. Her hand hesitated above the door-knob, and the sound came again. She recognized the low, almost inaudible murmur of a man's voice, punctuated by a tiny, muffled sob. There was another murmur of voices, and without conscious thought about what she was doing, Cathryn twisted the handle and quietly eased open the door.

The sight that met her eyes froze her feet to the door-step. Danielle Hunt was stretched out on the bed, her arms clasped possessively around Joshua's neck. She was facing the door, but it was unlikely that she saw Cathryn, for her eyes were swollen and blurred by tears, and her attention was fixed on Cathryn's husband. Between hic-cuping sobs, she was gasping out her undying love for him.

"How could you have married her, Joshua?" she murmured in an agonized whisper. "You know how we feel about each other. How could you do this to us?"

"Danielle, you're married to my father, for God's sake. What did you expect me to do? Besides, you loved him when you married him. You have to remember those feelings and forget about . . . what happened later."

"I only loved him because I hadn't met you."

With sick fascination, Cathryn watched Joshua stroke the hair out of his stepmother's eyes. She could almost feel the gentleness of his touch.

"That's not true, Danielle, I'm sure of it."

"You don't love *her,* do you, Joshua?" She clutched feverishly at his jacket. "Tell me you don't love her. You only married her because you were desperate to put another barrier between us. That was why you did it, wasn't it?"

Very quietly, as quietly as she had opened it, Cathryn shut the bedroom door. She bent down, picked up her suitcase, and walked back down the stairs. When she reached the front door, she bumped into it.

She stared incomprehendingly at the solid panel of the front door, then placed her suitcase neatly to one side of the entrance. She turned around and walked in the opposite direction, weaving slightly from side to side, as if she were drunk. When she came to another door barring her path, she pushed it open and found herself in the kitchen.

The cleaning lady was standing at the draining board scraping carrots.

"Well hello again, Mrs. Hunt. Did you get your suitcase unpacked?" She gave an inoffensive little chuckle. "Two Mr. Hunts and two Mrs. Hunts in one household. It's a bit much, isn't it?"

"Yes, it certainly is." Cathryn heard the edge of hysteria in her voice and forced it back. "Please call me Cathryn," she said.

"And my name's Barb. Would you like a glass of iced tea? There's a jug in the fridge, if you do. I'd pour it out for you, but I've been chopping onions."

"I prefer lemon in my tea," Cathryn said. "Not onions."

"Mrs. Hunt... Cathryn... are you all right? You look a bit pale, if you don't mind me saying so."

"I'm fine. Terrific." She turned blindly toward the refrigerator and bumped straight into Joshua.

"Cathy! Darling! I spotted your suitcase in the hall, but I thought I must be hallucinating." He swept her into his arms, kissing her fiercely. "Mmm... I've missed you."

"Have you?" Her bones felt as if they had turned to steel, she was so unyielding in his arms, and her skin burned with the acid force of her rejection. Only her heart betrayed her, skittering with a foolish urgency because his smiles seemed so devastatingly sincere. He looked at her strangely when she spoke, as if sensing her resistance and silently questioning the reason.

She said nothing, unable to think of any words bitter enough to express the depth of her hurt, and he bent to kiss her again. Catching the lingering scent of Danielle's perfume on his shirt, she jerked her head away, afraid she might be physically sick.

His tender smile disappeared, and his arms fell back to his sides. He walked to the sink and poured a glass of water, drinking it down quickly.

"What are you doing here?" he asked coolly. "I thought you were supposed to be away all week."

"Yes, I'm sure you did." She felt Barb's curiosity and the intensity of Joshua's hard, probing stare. Breathing deeply, she forced herself to appear calm. She had long experience in disguising her inner distress, but it didn't seem to be helping her now.

"Mr. Marlowe, our senior partner, gave me an extra week's vacation," she said as evenly as she could. She looked up, unable to prevent some of her tumultuous emotions from showing. "He seemed to think we'd both enjoy an extension of our honeymoon."

"I see."

Even the pretense of calm was suddenly too much for Cathryn. "I'm really tired, Joshua," she said. "I'd like to take a shower and rest for a little while before dinner. Shouldn't you be back at the office? What are you doing home on a Monday afternoon?"

"I left some papers in my bedroom. I wasn't sure where I'd put them, or I'd have sent somebody else to pick them up. But you're right, I ought to get back to the office."

"Then I'll see you this evening, I guess."

She hurried out of the kitchen before he could say anything to detain her. She rushed upstairs to his room, hating to enter it knowing that Danielle had been there, but unable to think of where else to go. She banged the door shut and locked it.

She felt dirty, soiled, and humiliated to the depths of her soul. How dare Joshua marry her when he was in love with someone else? She started to strip off her clothes, which seemed to her heightened senses to smell of Danielle's perfume. She tore viciously at the buttons of her blouse, not caring when several of them ripped off and scattered about the room. How could she have been so blind? How could she have missed so many clues as to the true state of Joshua's feelings?

Because he had lied to her. Deliberately deceived her. Betrayed her.

She was down to her bra and bikini briefs, pacing up and down the room, too angry even to get into the shower, when Joshua came in.

"How did you get in here?" she demanded, grabbing a towel from a chair and wrapping it under her arms. Hurt, fury, and grief churned inside her, making her almost incoherent with anger.

"Through the door."

"It was locked. I locked it."

"It's one of those modern latches. It's designed to open from either side."

"Now, there's an interesting new concept in locks! It's like a modern marriage, I suppose. Not meant to put any restraints on anybody. Convenient or purposeless, depending on your point of view."

"What is it, Cathy? What's happened? What are you trying to tell me?"

He sounded genuinely concerned, and she hated him for his skill at pretending to care for her. He reached out to stroke the hollow between her breasts, and she jumped away from his touch as if his fingers carried venom in their tips. "Don't touch me," she said. "Don't ever touch me again."

"Why not?" His question was dangerously quiet. "You're my wife and I like touching you."

"As much as you like touching your stepmother?"

He exhaled in a long, low sigh. "You saw Danielle with me this afternoon." It was a statement, not a question.

"Yes, I saw you. I apologize for not having telephoned in advance to warn everyone I was coming. If I'd fully understood the situation, believe me, I wouldn't have embarrassed us all by arriving unannounced."

His expression was grim as he approached her, and Cathryn instinctively stepped back. Joshua stopped dead in his tracks as soon as he saw what she was doing. "I'm sorry you found out this way," he said. "I intended telling you the truth the next time we were alone together."

Her heart was slowly shattering into a thousand brittle pieces. "At least I've saved you the trouble of an embarrassing confession. Tell me, Joshua, why did you marry me?"

"For at least a dozen different reasons, most of which I didn't understand at the time. Listen, Cathy, things aren't the way they seem. I think you're probably leaping to all sorts of unfounded conclusions."

"You mean I imagined seeing you and Danielle on this bed? You mean you and your stepmother aren't committing adultery?"

Joshua flinched. "Danielle and I have never had any physical relationship whatsoever," he said quietly. His forced calm momentarily deserted him. "For heaven's sake, Cathy, she's my father's wife!"

"You were kissing her this afternoon. Isn't that a physical relationship? Or maybe you consider your kisses a purely spiritual experience."

"This afternoon was a mistake," he said tersely.

"Well, I'd certainly agree with that! How many other mistakes have there been, Joshua?"

There was a short, tense pause. "As soon as I . . . as soon as we realized how we felt about each other, we took care never to be alone."

"How honorable!" Cathryn ground out, unable to bear

his answer now that she had it. "And precisely how did our marriage fit into this cozy little love triangle? Don't tell me; let me guess. I was going to be your excuse for leaving home. No wonder you wanted us to get married quickly!"

He looked away. "That's not true. By the time I married you, my feelings for Danielle had changed."

"Oh sure! I saw this afternoon how your feelings for her had changed." Her short burst of laughter sounded dangerously like a sob. She swung away, holding her hand against her mouth.

"My God! I think I must have been walking around with blinkers on. That weekend by the beach ... Danielle expected to find you alone at the cottage, didn't she?"

"Maybe. I don't know. Yes, I guess she did." He took another step toward her, then held back when she instinctively recoiled.

"Cathy, please listen to me—really listen—while I try to explain what happened. Danielle and I got to know each other under exceptional circumstances. She was married to my father, but because of his constant traveling, she was spending most of her time alone in this house with me. She's pretty and she has a sweet nature; in fact, she's the epitome of traditional feminine virtues, the exact opposite of the sort of aggressive, ambitious women I meet every day in my work."

"You mean career women like me, I suppose?"

"No. That's not what I mean."

"I can certainly see how attractive Danielle would be as a prospective wife. She can cook, she creates a wonderful home atmosphere, and she's a charming hostess." Cathryn tried to cover the gnawing pain in her heart with a sophisticated smile. "How frustrating it must have been for you to find your perfect spouse had already been snapped up by your father! I'm surprised you didn't suggest a quick trip to Reno and a convenient divorce."

"I never even considered the possibility of marrying

Danielle. Neither of us would ever betray my father's trust."

"What were you doing this afternoon, Joshua? Finding a way to express your loyalty?"

He paled, and she saw him grit his teeth with the effort of keeping his temper. "Danielle came to say a final good-bye, and things got a little out of control."

"You have such a neat, understated way of expressing things." Her cool sarcasm contrasted dramatically with the tumultuous state of her emotions. What was actually tearing her apart, she realized, was the knowledge that Joshua didn't love her. That he had never loved her. That he had lied in order to persuade her to marry him. Her hurt boiled over into a furious, cold anger. "Precisely why did you marry me?" she asked with deadly calm.

"When I first met you, I'd already decided that the best way out of the whole horrible mess was for me to get married."

"And I was simply the lucky lady you happend to pick on?"

"Dammit, Cathy, that's not the way it was!" He drew a deep breath, once again forcing himself back under control. "When I met you, I knew I would never find a more suitable wife or a more perfect companion. It seemed to me that we had a very good chance of being happy together."

"So why did you lie to me?" Her voice faded to a whisper. "When you asked me to marry you, you said you loved me."

"I tried to be as honest with you as I could, but you didn't want to hear the truth."

"What do you mean? Of course I wanted the truth!"

"You wanted to marry me." His contradiction sounded slightly weary. "You wanted me to coerce you into marriage so that you could come to me without admitting exactly what you'd done. Be honest with yourself, Cathy, or we'll never get anything settled between us. We both wanted to share our lives. We both wanted children. We both wanted to settle down in a permanent home. We liked each other. We were already good friends. But you wanted to throw away our chance of real happiness because you were in love with a dead man."

"So you lied to me."

"Yes, I lied to you! I lied because I thought you were being unreasonable. You were in love with Robert. God knows, you told me often enough that you would never love anyone else. I thought I would never love any woman other than Danielle. It seemed to me that we were ideally suited—two people who would never hurt each other because their emotions weren't deeply involved and never would be. So I lied. I told an untruth! Is that an unforgivable crime? I offered you the words of love you said you wanted." He turned away. "If you like, I'll admit now that I was wrong, but it seemed the simplest thing to do at the time."

"I'll bet it did! And how do you suppose I feel, knowing that you picked me out as a suitable brood mare to hatch your children?"

For a second, a faint smile lightened his grim expression. "I think your metaphors are getting a bit mixed. Brood mares don't hatch their offspring."

"Don't patronize me!"

His expression hardened. "All right, I won't. Let's stop shouting about my motives and discuss your motives. Are you sure they're absolutely crystal pure? I'd say that sexually you were a pretty frustrated woman by the time I came along. In case you think I haven't noticed, I'm well aware of the fact that you like having sex with me. Robert may be your one and only true love, but I sure as hell make a great substitute in bed. Why is it all right for you to marry me because I'm an acceptable stud, but not all right for me to marry you because you make a good mother and an entertaining friend?"

"How dare you!"

"How dare I what? Tell you that you're hot in bed?"

She was too badly hurt to accept any part of his explanation. After eighteen months of repression, she had just started to feel deep emotions again, and she shouted at Joshua with all the pent up frustration of weeks of confusion. "You had no right to lie to me! No right at all! You tricked me into marrying you."

"You'd better stop screaming unless you want everybody in the house to know what we're fighting about."

"They'll know soon enough when I file for divorce. Which I plan to do right now, if not slightly sooner."

She stormed over to the closet and threw the door open, then remembered that her suitcase was still packed and waiting downstairs. She marched to the bedroom door, only to find Joshua blocking her exit.

"Let me through! I'm leaving."

"Dressed in a towel? Do me a favor, Cathy, and shut up long enough to hear what I'm saying. My relationship with Danielle—such as it was—is over. It's through. It's finished. This whole scene is pointless."

"Pointless!" Cathryn had to stop to draw in a gulp of air. As soon as she had breath in her lungs, she opened her mouth to hurl another angry remark at Joshua, but whatever she had been going to say was swallowed up in his kiss. His lips came down and seized hers with apparently tormented passion, his tongue forcing its way deep into her mouth.

For a moment she struggled, but she knew her resistance was without real meaning. Despite everything she had learned about the true state of Joshua's feelings, she still wanted him to make love to her. She heard the pounding of her own blood in her ears as he tightened his arms around her, moving his lips from her mouth down the long, slender line of her throat to her breasts. His burning hands moved over her, ripping away the towel and her underclothes as he rained kisses over her entire body.

Her legs began to weaken, and suddenly they were both on the floor, her head cushioned on their discarded clothing. Joshua's hands continued their fiery seduction, and as her body melted into passion, he murmured little words of love, praising her beauty, telling her how wonderful she was as a lover. Cathryn heard her own low moan of longing and wondered despairingly how her body could respond so readily to him after all she had learned about his feelings. The truth was, she realized with a final, despairing flash of rationality, that when Joshua made love to her, it was impossible to believe that he could be in love with anyone else. His involvement, his tenderness, and his passion all seemed totally for her.

She wrapped her arms tightly around his neck, sealing her body to his. His kiss flared into the final blaze of passion, and she surrendered to him in the total submission that gave them both victory. For a brief, glorious moment, it was enough.

Chapter Eleven

THEY WERE STILL lying silently in each other's arms, hazy with the afterglow of passion, when a knock sounded on the bedroom door.

"Mr. Hunt? Are you there?"

He sat up slowly, rested on one elbow, and ran a hand through his tousled hair. "Yes, Barb. I'm here."

"Isn't the phone in your bedroom working? There's a call for you on your business line from Merchant National Bank in California."

"I don't think the phone rang in here. Thanks for the message, Barb. I'll come right now."

Joshua got up, pulling Cathryn to her feet. He looked at her without saying anything, his expression strangely hesitant.

"Your bank's waiting to talk to you," she said finally.

"Yes. It'll be about the cash I'm trying to raise for that movie." He shrugged into his robe. "But I'll be right back. Will you wait here for me?"

She gave him a vague, noncommittal smile, then scarcely waited for the door to close behind him before pulling on her discarded clothes. She hoped his call would last long enough for her to make good her escape, but she seemed to be all thumbs as she tried to hook her bra. Earlier, in her anger, she had torn off so many buttons from her muslin shirt that it wouldn't stay fastened. Impatiently, she tied it in a knot beneath her breasts, hoping that it looked merely casual, not totally indecent.

She slipped out of the house, not bothering to take her suitcase, which was far too heavy to carry. She ran to the end of the long driveway, then plodded down the leafy country lane for almost a mile until she reached a small gas station. The pay phone was functioning, and she called for a cab, staring blankly out of the grimy gas station until it arrived. Luck, if she could consider it that, was still with her when the cab drew up at the train station. The express for New York was scheduled to arrive within five minutes.

She didn't think much on the journey back to Manhattan. Listening to the rhythmic clacking of the train wheels on the track, she felt soothed by the monotony of the sound. When she got back to her apartment, she stripped off her clothes and immediately stepped into the shower. The hot water was almost too refreshing. Her brain was reactivated as soon as the spray hit her.

At first she was able to convince herself that she had left Connecticut simply because she needed time to herself, away from Joshua. She needed to work out what she was going to do next, although it was obvious that the only sensible thing was to file for divorce. How could she endure living with Joshua, loving him, knowing he was in love with someone else? His stepmother, of all people.

She shuddered and turned off the shower, feeling more than a little sick. She dried herself quickly and rummaged through her closet until she found a silky robe the color of rich yellow cream. She pulled the lapels across her chest and tied the belt tightly around her waist so that virtually every inch of her skin was covered. Some analytic and tiresomely honest part of her brain immediately pointed out that her belt tightening had merely stretched the fabric provocatively over the swell of her breasts and the curve of her hips. She glanced in the steamy bathroom mirror and realized that she had made herself look like an exciting, shiny gift package waiting to be unwrapped.

But nobody wanted to unwrap the gift—certainly not Joshua. Maybe he wanted her body, but he certainly didn't want the love and the other emotions that went along with it. She switched on the television, then switched it off even before the image stabilized on the screen. She poured out a drink, but poured it down the sink without tasting it. She selected a book from her shelves, then tossed it onto the sofa unopened.

Pacing up and down her living room, she forced herself to acknowledge the truth. She hadn't run away from Joshua because she wanted solitude. She hadn't needed time to think. She had run away because she wanted him to follow her. She wanted proof that he cared. She wanted him to burst into the apartment, sweep her into his arms, and proclaim his undying love for her. She wanted him to say that he had never really loved Danielle, that he loved only her. Cathryn stopped her restless pacing long enough to laugh hollowly at her own foolishness.

Suddenly her forehead felt feverishly hot, and she leaned it against the cool plaster of her apartment wall. Oh, Joshua, she thought, why did I have to fall in love with you? I swore I would never let myself be hurt like this again. I don't want to feel this kind of pain, not anymore.

She heard the sound of a key turning in the lock of her front door, and her heart gave an unguarded leap of hope. The door was pushed partway open.

"Will you take off the chain so I can come in?" Joshua asked quietly.

Her fingers shook as she removed the safety chain. He wasn't storming in and sweeping her off her feet, but at least he was here.

He stepped into the apartment, bolting the door behind him, then leaned against it, making no effort to come farther into the room. To her surprise, she saw that he looked pale, almost gray, beneath the healthy glow of his tan. Unfortunately for her thudding heart, despite his pallor he still appeared as devastatingly attractive as ever.

"Running away isn't going to solve anything," he said finally. "Can't we at least talk things over? Won't you let me explain about Danielle?"

"I don't know," she said. "Some explanations hurt too much. Sometimes it's better just to accept that everything's over."

His expression hardened. "Why should everything be over between us? I thought we both cared for each other, at least as friends..."

"I don't think of you as my friend." Although she tried to speak normally, the confession emerged as little more than a husky whisper. She looked down at her fingers and discovered they were rolling and unrolling her satin belt. She tried to think of something else to do with them, but there didn't seem to be anywhere to put them. Eventually, in desperation, she clasped them around her body and raised her eyes to her husband.

He was gazing at her breasts. Her nipples hardened reflexively against the silky fabric. At last his glance fell away, and he thrust his hands into the pockets of his jeans, staring down fixedly at the floor.

"I'm sorry you don't consider me a friend," he said. "I guess I ruined everything by not being honest with you, but I was afraid to take the risk." His voice was strained. "Cathy, we have so much going for us. Aren't you willing to give our marriage another try?"

"You're asking rather a lot, Joshua. A marriage without love has no reserves to draw on in a crisis, whatever else it may have going for it."

"In the last century they used to claim love came after marriage, not before."

"How can we expect love to grow between us when you're in love with another woman? There's no need for you to keep up that sordid pretense any longer, Joshua. We both married strictly for practical reasons. The only difference between us is that I was honest about my reasons. You weren't."

"I'm not sure either of us was completely honest."

"All you wanted was a barrier between you and your stepmother, something that would protect your father's marriage."

"And what did you want, Cathryn?"

"I wanted a home and somebody to be a father for my children. I've told you that at least a dozen times."

"Then why did you run away from me? If all you want from, our marriage is a home and children, I'm more than willing to offer you both those things. According to your logic, we're both getting just what we wanted, so there's no sensible reason for you to run away."

She turned and walked quickly to the sofa, angry at her unconscious self-betrayal. She sat down, drumming her fingers nervously on the back of the sofa. "I ran away because you deceived me," she said. "I was honest with you. I told you I was in love with Robert, but you lied to me about Danielle."

"I lied to you in the beginning," he said slowly, "but by the time we were married, the only person I was deceiving was myself. I wasn't looking for love when I asked you to marry me, but I found it anyway."

Her heart gave a little leap of hope, but she steeled herself against it. "You sound very convincing, Joshua," she said cynically. "But then you always did."

"Maybe that's because I was telling you more of the truth than I ever knew. Cathy, if I hadn't been so determined to ignore my own feelings, I'd have recognized what I felt for you right from the start. I must have met at least a dozen eligible single women since I first imagined I was in love with Danielle. I didn't pursue any of them. I certainly didn't come up with crazy schemes to coerce them into marriage at the first available opportunity."

She pushed away another flash of hope that twisted her heart. "Imagined yourself in love with Danielle? What does that mean?"

He sat down beside her on the sofa, leaving a tiny space between her satin-clad knee and his denim-covered thigh. "I told you this afternoon how it was. Danielle is one of the prettiest women I've ever met. She's a devoted homemaker. She was longing to be a mother, and I felt protective toward her when she miscarried. I suppose, in some ways, I really did love her for a while."

"But now you're convinced your feelings of love were all imagination? I'm not sure I find that very reassuring, Joshua."

"It's not that my feelings for Danielle weren't real. But since I met you, I've realized that what I felt for her was no more than a shadow of real love. Most of what I was feeling was sympathy because she had such a rotten time for the first few months of her marriage. I realize now that if Danielle and I had ever married, we'd have driven each other crazy before we got back from our honeymoon."

Joshua moved along the sofa until the tiny gap between them disappeared. His hand trailed hypnotically up and down her thigh. "Whereas with you . . ."

"Whereas with me the sexual attraction has outlasted the honeymoon. Hooray!"

"What I feel for you is a hell of a lot more than sexual

attraction." He took her hands in his, grasping them tightly and stopping her nervous thrumming. "Cathy, I'll be totally honest with you even though I'm probably not doing myself any favors by telling the truth. As soon as I realized how I felt about Danielle, I started to date a different woman every night in an effort to put her out of my mind. The first time I asked you out, you were simply one more in a string of dates that was already beginning to seem endless. I'm not proud of the way I behaved, but I thought if I slept with enough different women, I'd eventually be able to forget my stepmother. I used to play a mental game with myself, calculating how many hours I'd need to spend with my latest date at a restaurant or a bar or a disco before she'd agree to come with me to some motel."

The memory of their first meeting flashed into Cathryn's mind. "You mean you escorted me back to the hotel that first night as part of some crude bet with yourself?"

He actually blushed. "I admit it sounds pretty despicable. But, Cathy, nothing worked out the way I'd planned. We stopped outside your room, and I went into my regular good night routine. I started to kiss you, and it seemed like the walls of the motel had collapsed on top of me. I'd almost forgotten what it felt like to experience real desire for a woman, but as soon as I took you into my arms, my libido went into immediate overdrive."

"You certainly hid your feelings effectively. You never even tried to get an invitation into my room."

The beginnings of a smile touched his mouth. "You sound cross that I didn't try to seduce you, Cathy, my love. You're supposed to be flattered."

"Don't call me that. I'm not your love."

"Yes you are. My one and only love." He put his arm around her shoulders and tilted up her chin with his other hand. "I love you, Cathryn."

"Last month you loved Danielle."

"No. I'd already met you last month." He laughed without humor. "You know, every time I asked you out, I swore it was going to be the last time. I even avoided making love to you for as long as I could stand it. I was afraid of what I might find out about my own feelings once we became lovers."

"Is that why—the first time we made love—you seemed almost relieved when I... when I..."

"Stopped responding? Yes. I wasn't ready to admit that making love to you had practically knocked my socks off."

"They were already off," she said.

His eyes warmed with laughter. "Oh, Cathy, what I feel for you is so much stronger and more powerful than anything I've ever felt before, I can't imagine trying to face life without you. I love you in every way a man can possibly love a woman. Please say you'll give our marriage another chance."

She forced herself to ignore the soft, melting sensation his words evoked. "How do you know your love for me won't disappear overnight? According to you, that's more or less what happened to your feelings for Danielle."

"This is different. Once you've really been in love, you can never mistake the feeling again." His eyes were suddenly shadowed with pain. "You love Robert, so you ought to know how unmistakable it is. God knows you've told me about your feelings for him often enough."

"Are you jealous, Joshua?" she asked softly.

"Yes, dammit! I'm jealous." His mouth tightened into another grim smile. "Humiliating, isn't it, to be sick with envy of a man who's been dead for nearly two years."

She resisted the impulse to reach up and kiss the lips that hovered so close to hers. "I'll always love Robert," she said. "He was a wonderful man. But that doesn't mean I'll never love anybody else. I guess I've learned recently that love can grow."

She sensed the absolute stillness in him. "Cathy, what are you saying?"

She trailed her fingers along his waist, pausing at the buckle of his belt while she gathered courage to make the confession. "That first time you made love to me ... I only stopped responding because it seemed disloyal to Robert's memory to want you so much. I still want you, Joshua. I've wanted you almost from the first moment we met."

His arms tightened convulsively around her, and she leaned toward him, her robe gaping deliberately, tantalizingly open. He kissed her as if he had been starving and she was a sudden, unexpected source of nourishment.

"Make love to me, Joshua," she whispered.

He rested his palm against the curve of her cheek and slowly ran it back to smooth her hair away from her eyes. She felt his fingers tremble against her skin as she lay back on the sofa, pulling him down on top of her. She felt the aching hunger in him as he touched his mouth to her hair, her eyes, and finally her lips. She felt his love in every stroke of his body, and in the end there seemed to be no reason not to tell him the truth hidden in her heart.

"I love you, Joshua," she said, and the words seemed to flow out of her mouth into his. "I love you so much that it hurts."

His eyes flared with sudden fierce emotion, and he cupped her chin, pressing his mouth urgently to hers. "Tell me again," he breathed. "Oh, Cathy, I thought I might never hear you say that."

"I want you. I need you. I love you."

He captured her hands and held them over her head as his mouth descended with crushing force against hers. Their bodies blazed into life together and the fire consumed them, burning away the last, lingering shadows of doubt. She fell asleep curled up in his arms, only dreamily aware of the moment when he lifted her from the sofa and carried her to bed.

She didn't wake up until the first pink light of dawn poked through a narrow gap in the bedroom drapes. Twisting her head on the pillow, she discovered Joshua was already awake, propped up on one arm, looking down at her with eyes misted with love. Simultaneously, she realized that not only the sunlight had awakened her. Joshua was trailing his hands enticingly over her stomach.

She sat up. "What are you doing?" she asked huskily.

He grinned, pushing her back gently against the pillows. "Preparing to make babies," he said. "I found a seventeenth-century medical textbook in a rare-book store recently and it has a recipe in it that's guaranteed to produce twins. They even promised that with enough effort, you could produce 'one of the male sex and one who is female.'"

His fingers continued to weave erotic patterns. "Do we ... er ... do we actually want twins?" she managed to ask.

"Why not? If this book is right, we may have discovered a whole new approach to instant families." He bent his head and pressed a complicated swirl of kisses against the underside of her breasts. "And if the book is wrong, think what fun we'll have testing the recipe. So far, you've only experienced a preliminary sample of the treats in store."

She closed her eyes for a moment, opening them again when her body began to quiver with pleasure. "In the interest of medical science, I'm prepared to endure anything," she murmured.

He smiled with the supreme confidence of a man who knows he is loved. "For that remark, my dear Cathryn, you will be rewarded with a first-hand opportunity to try my seventeenth-century recipe for producing quadruplets. Believe me, it has some very interesting variations."

She reached up, linking her hands behind his neck

and drawing his mouth down to hers. "I love you," she said. "And do you know what? I have a great idea. Let's start with the regular, run-of-the-mill method for producing one baby at a time and gradually work up to quads as we get the hang of it."

"That seems very faint-hearted," he said reprovingly. "Think how long it will take before we get to try for quintuplets."

"But, Josh, we have the rest of our lives to perfect our technique."

His breath came out on a sigh of contentment, and he gathered her tightly into his arms. "Yes," he said. "We have the rest of our lives to spend together, a lifetime to show you how much I love you."

"No more talking," she said. "Just show me."